Dedication

To all those who have served.

Her Relentless SEAL

Midnight Delta Series
Book 10

A Novel

By Caitlyn O'Leary

Edited by Lynne St. James
Cover by Croco Designs

SYNOPSIS

ON THE RUN FOR HER LIFE

Small-town girl Evie Avery's dream vacation has become her worst nightmare. Now she's on the run in a foreign country and has no idea why.

NO ROOM FOR ERROR

Navy SEAL, Aiden O'Malley, had his reasons for turning his back on Evie all those months ago, but he hasn't been able to get her out of his mind. She changed him, for better or worse. When he finds out she's missing, long pent-up feelings come roaring to life, and he will stop at nothing to bring her home.

A LOVE WORTH FIGHTING FOR

Evie finds herself face-to-face with a man she vowed to forget. The flame she thought had burned out months ago suddenly ignites. Storming back to Tennessee, she is mad as hell when he follows her. Worse, she finds that the terror she'd experienced abroad is still stalking her. Aiden hounds Evie's every step as he tries to keep her alive, but she doesn't care. It's not his protection she wants. If she can't have his heart, she wants him gone. As the enemy closes in, Aiden wonders if there is enough of his battered soul to give to a woman who deserves the world.

Chapter One

Present Day – Antakya - Turkey

See the world, he said.

You'll have fun, he said.

It'll be the time of your life, he said.

Evie ran faster, still unable to believe that she was being chased by a man with a gun. This was not going to end well.

Think, Avery, think.

He was a native. Meanwhile, a white girl running through a bazaar in Antakya, Turkey, was just screaming for attention.

Up ahead she saw the shop she'd visited quite often in the last few days. She made a beeline for it. She hated to bring trouble to Zehra and Nehir, but it was a matter of life and death.

Hers.

"Evie!" Nehir greeted her as she ran through the opening of their rug shop. Evie lost no time scrambling under one of the large carpets on the floor and covering herself up. She knew how smart the women were, having spent hours with them. She tried to keep her breathing shallow and control her shudders so that the thick material above her would not move and betray her hiding place.

She could hear raised voices in Turkish. After a week in Turkey, she could easily identify the language and was proud she could even speak a few phrases. But there wasn't a chance in hell she could actually understand them. Evie clenched her hands in frustration.

If she had to guess, the guy with the gun was asking where the bitch of an American woman was. She hoped that Zehra and Nehir would not give her away. Please say sisterhood would win out over nationality.

The man continued to yell, then she heard him coming further into the narrow confines of the shop. He stomped past where she was hidden on the floor. She prayed like she'd never prayed before.

Shit, shit, shit.

Was her phone on vibrate? No, she knew it wasn't.

She eased the zipper of her fanny pack open and felt for her smart phone, then eased the tab over to the vibrate setting. Sweat coated her back despite the fact it was only sixty degrees. She still hadn't wrapped her head around the fact that she could be in the Middle East and it was chillier than in Tennessee.

Dammit, why couldn't she be home right now? Why had she ever wanted to go on an adventure? What had she been thinking?

* * *

Same Day – Undisclosed Location

"Is he going to make it?" Mason demanded.

"If we can get him to the ship in time." Aiden didn't look up from his patient. He was one of three men that they had rescued from a place that didn't exist in a country that they should never have been in.

Aiden had no clue what idiot in their company had told these three oil executives that they would be safe there, but they should be strung up by their thumbs.

Anybody who read a newspaper would have known that this region was a volatile mess, and any American there was likely risking their life. Now Aiden and his SEAL team were there to yank their asses out of the fire.

This man had ripped open his stomach when he'd botched an escape attempt and tried to climb through a torn steel-mesh fence. His wound had been festering for over a day, according to his colleagues. Now Aiden was using everything at his disposal to keep the guy together for the helicopter extraction. He tore the duct tape with his teeth and wrapped it around they guy's abdomen over the sterile gauze covering the gash on his stomach. They needed to get him to a surgeon ASAP.

The man groaned in pain.

Damn!

The cocktail of antibiotics and painkillers that Aiden had given him should have kept him out cold.

"We need to move. Speed it up."

He didn't spare Mason a glance. Aiden knew that they must have gotten some hairy sucking intel if his lieutenant was stating the obvious. He grabbed the remaining supplies and bloody gauze. Just as he was hoisting his patient, his teammate, Drake Avery, materialized at his side. No matter how much animosity the man might harbor against Aiden off-hours, he was always a professional on the job.

"Together," was all Drake said as he helped to heft the man upward.

Despite the fact that they were gentle, he gave a weak shriek and went limp.

Thank God.

"Dumb son of a bitch. Gary's going to end up getting us killed. Can't we leave him behind?" one of the two other evacuees complained loudly.

"We'll get all of you home safely," Mason assured the man.

Aiden was impressed with Mason's calm response. He might agree that Gary was an idiot, but there was no way on God's green earth that a SEAL would ever leave a man behind.

"What an asshole," Drake muttered.

Aiden gave a small nod of agreement.

A half-mile later, he noted that the same man who'd complained was having a hard time keeping up with them. Figured. Aiden started counting in his head, knowing what was coming next. He hadn't even reached thirty when the expected question came.

"How much longer?" Aiden winced at the man's petulant tone.

"Seven more miles," Mason answered.

"Why couldn't they land the helicopter closer to where we were?" the man whined.

"We need to get over those hills up ahead. It's a safer place for the helicopters to land."

"We have to go over those hills?" the man gasped.

"We need to start moving faster. The pick-up is in one and a half hours," Mason said.

"That's impossible," the executive said.

"If we can make it, you can make it," Drake bit out.

Dumbass would want somebody to carry him before it was all over, Aiden thought to himself.

Darius, another team member, slowed down so that he was beside Aiden.

"Want me to take over?" he asked, nodding to the unconscious man Aiden was carrying.

"I'm good," Aiden answered.

"Drake?" Darius asked.

Drake laughed softly and shook his head. Darius fell back further to join Aiden's two other team members, Jack and Clint, who were bringing up the rear with the two businessmen.

"When can we stop?" It was the same man as before.

"We can't. Here, have some water," Darius said.

"I'm not going to make it."

"Shut up, Ed. Just keep your fucking mouth shut and your feet moving, and we might make it out of here alive."

It was the first time Aiden had heard the third evacuee talk. It turned out he liked the man.

"George, I'll report you to Kevin for insubordination."

Aiden chuckled, and it mingled with the rest of the team's laughter.

"Are you for real?" Drake asked incredulously. "Dude, stand down and listen to your friend with a brain."

"Avery," Mason said warningly.

Aiden understood Mason cautioning Drake. Aiden admired the fact that their lieutenant ran a tight ship. Mason believed in treating the people under his care with the utmost respect, no matter how much they might provoke the SEAL team members. But God knew this asshat was certainly putting them all to the test.

"We're going to need to get a move on," Clint said suddenly.

Aiden knew that he was the team member in charge of communications. Clint had either heard from one of the pilots, or he'd heard something from the building they had just left behind.

"How much time do we have?" Mason asked from the front of the formation.

"Our window is now forty-five minutes," Clint responded.

Aiden glanced at the men behind him, and, even in the moonlight, he could see that they were wearing dress shoes. The man named George caught his eye.

"I'm good. I run triathlons." He wasn't short of breath.

Darius and Jack got on either side of Ed.

"If you need any help making it, Sir, I can help you," Jack said in a Texas twang.

"You can do this, Ed. We can make it," Aiden heard George encourage his co-worker.

Mason looked at him and Drake. "You two good?" They nodded.

Taking point, he jogged up the slope of the hill, and they followed in his footsteps. Aiden hated jostling the injured man, but he had done everything possible to ensure that he could survive the trip to the evacuation point. Now they just had to make it there in time to meet their transport and get the hell out of Dodge.

There was a commotion from behind.

"I've got him," Jack said.

Aiden didn't turn. He needed all of his focus on making it up the hill, but he surmised that Ed had faltered or fallen, and Jack was now carting his ass. They were heading into a wooded area, and Mason increased his pace, but carefully picked through the underbrush, so that the team could handle their loads without making a misstep.

The man in his grasp started to struggle.

"Help!" he screamed, and twisted violently, then he let out a shrill scream. He was delirious.

Goddammit!

"Sir, I need you to calm down."

"Hurts," he gasped.

Aiden looked down and saw that blood was dripping out from under the duct tape. There was a lot. He wasn't going to make it if he didn't bind him up tighter.

"Mason, we've got to stop," Drake said.

"Can't," Mason said.

"No other option," Aiden told his commander.

Mason paused. "Darius, lead the others to the rendezvous point."

"Nope, you go too, Mase. Aiden and I have this," Drake said.

"Wrong. He's my patient. I have this. You all go. I'll bring him with me."

"He's never going to make it if you try to carry him over your shoulder, and you know it. If you carry him in your arms, you won't make it there in time. Face it, you're stuck with me." Drake glared at him, daring him to disagree.

Aiden assessed the man who had been giving him nothing but hell for the last two months and finally nodded in agreement. Both he and Drake looked at Mason simultaneously.

"I expect you two to be at the rendezvous point on time, and I expect this man to be alive."

"Done," Drake said.

"Affirmative," Aiden answered, already pulling at the makeshift bandage to assess the damage, as he shrugged out of his backpack. Drake, meanwhile, had a flashlight shining on the gaping wound.

The other men filed past, and Aiden saw that Jack was indeed carrying the man who'd been complaining. He pulled out his medical supplies and went to work.

Bloody! Fucking! Hell! *Mierda*! *Diu*! Aiden continued to swear mentally in English, Mandarin, Spanish, Arabic, Cantonese, and Mayan.

"Close it up. We've got to go."

Aiden looked up at Drake. He'd been monitoring the time. Aiden knew that the man had given him as much time as possible. He didn't think it was enough. But he stopped swearing and started praying as he closed the gaping wound for the last time.

"Hurts," the man, named Gary, said again. He'd been crying out in pain for the last agonizing six minutes.

"I can't give you anything more for pain. We're going to carry you to the helicopters, and it's going to hurt even more, but we need you to hold still, okay?" Aiden asked the man as he and Drake lifted him up.

The man let out a long gasp. "Okay," he whispered.

Aiden and Drake ran.

They heard the helicopters before they saw them.

Mason and Darius were on the top of the ridge, waiting for them.

"We've got him," Mason commanded. "Go."

He and Drake didn't hesitate. They transferred the man, and made a beeline for the helicopters. A man was hanging out of the one closest to them, urging them toward him. They jumped aboard. Clint was the only other SEAL aboard, and he'd already started setting up the pallet for the injured man.

"How is he?" Clint asked.

"Not good," Aiden said as he pulled out the saline to get ready for his patient. Clint pointed behind him, and he raced across the belly of the bird to assist the others in getting Gary into the helicopter. Gary was out cold, which was a blessing.

He and Drake worked fast to get him strapped in, then Aiden had the IV going and secured the blood pressure cuff around his arm. Gary's airway was good, but he had lost too much blood. He needed surgery. There wasn't any blood on the copter to give him a transfusion. Aiden read the blood pressure, it was shit.

"ETA?" Aiden demanded.

Mason was immediately beside him. "A little over an hour before we reach the ship."

Drake was pulling the survival blanket around Gary, and then a wool blanket on top of that.

Nobody asked him if the man was going to survive. They knew the odds as well as he did. They were abysmal, and there wasn't a damn thing more Aiden could do for him except pray. Maria Margarita Canul O'Malley would be over the moon if she knew just how often her son prayed.

CHAPTER TWO

Same Day – Antakya, Turkey

"Evie, he's gone."

It was Nehir. She was whispering as she repositioned one of the rugs, so it almost covered Evie.

"There are two other men walking through the bazaar. They, they..." Then Nehir started speaking in Turkish. She did that sometimes, as if Evie would understand her if she spoke slowly.

"Nehir, I don't understand what you're saying," Evie said slowly in English.

The woman flushed, clearly frustrated. "Not safe," she finally said. More thick carpets were piled on top of Evie. "Must stay." She held out her hand and put up four fingers. Evie knew that the shop closed in four more hours. Dammit, she had to pee.

"Call the police," Evie told her.

"No." She started talking fast in Turkish. It was clear what she was saying upset her.

"English," Evie interrupted.

"Mans are bad. No police," Nehir finally said.

Well, that cleared up nothing.

Evie heard women talking. Customers must have come into the shop. Zehra greeted them in Turkish. Hopefully, they wouldn't want the rugs she was hiding under.

Evie turned her head so the blue wool wasn't resting over her mouth and nose. The heavy material was making it hard to breathe. She pushed and created more of an air pocket. Thank God, she wasn't allergic to wool. She closed her eyes, and tried to remain calm, then opened them and took in the blue material. It reminded her of the skies of Tennessee. What was she doing in Turkey? Oh yeah, she was on an adventure with her bosses.

First Italy, then Greece, then Jim had gotten a wild hair to come to Turkey. How the hell he had gotten the visas was anyone's guess. Good to have friends in high places. They'd invited her along while the hotel she worked at was being renovated. They were good guys, and were trying to stop her moping around. But Jim had been acting hinky since they arrived five days ago. Then a seriously scary friend of his had shown up at their hotel last night, and Jim said he needed to go with him this morning on an errand. Alone.

Blake wasn't having any of it. There was no way he was letting his lover go with scary dude by himself. Of course, scary was relative since Jim was a former Army Ranger and Blake was a former Marine. Still, this guy pinged all of Evie's senses. The dude definitely seemed desperate.

She'd been happy that Blake had gone with Jim. That had left her in the hotel by herself, which was fine. She'd been having a blast going to the bazaar. Tomorrow they were due to fly back to the states, so today she was going to get souvenirs for her five sisters and one soon-to-be sister-in-law. Hell, she might even pick up something fun for her brother Drake.

It was when she was two blocks away from the hotel that the man with the gun had tried to grab her. She'd spent too many years evading her father's love taps to not know how to dodge and weave past this dumbass. Instinct had her running. It never occurred to her to call the cops. Hell, she didn't even know what the word for police or help was in Turkish. Her first damn impulse was to get to a friendly face and hide.

Stupid!

So stupid.

But maybe not. Nehir didn't want to call the police. Maybe her instincts were spot on. As soon as it was safe, she was going to call her badass bosses. They would get her out of this mess.

She fingered her fanny pack. It had been her big sister Trenda who had drilled it into her head that she needed to keep all her valuables with her at all times. This included her passport. So, right now she could go to the Embassy without a problem. If the police were out of the question, she needed to get to the American Embassy. She inched the carpet away to see if the coast was clear. Damn it. This time there was a couple in the shop. She eased the rug back over her face.

She heard voices; they were close. She felt some of the weight above her shift. Then Zehra was talking…fast. The material settled back down on top of her, collapsing her air pocket. She took a shallow breath, then another.

She heard footsteps, then she heard Nehir saying good-bye in Turkish. That was about all she understood of the language, hello, goodbye, please, and thank you. Evie took her shot and shifted the material so that she could breathe easier. Having trouble breathing took her mind off having to pee.

Pee.

Damn. She shouldn't have thought about that. Now her mind could only think about needing a bathroom. Even the dark cubicle in the public restrooms in the bazaar seemed like paradise.

Carefully, Evie crossed her legs under the rugs.

Suck it up, Avery. This is not the worst situation you've been in.

She breathed through her nose as memories bubbled upwards. She shoved them down.

Come on Evalyn Lavender Avery. You're a grown woman now. Now you handle things with a bat, remember? She grinned at that memory. She tried to think through what the hell had gotten her into this situation. Her gut told her this had something to do with scary guy. But Jim and Blake would save her. Between the two of them, they were probably five times her size. They would kick these guys' asses. That made her smile.

"Evie?" It was Nehir. The woman pushed back the carpet covering Evie. "We go."

She couldn't believe it. She must have dozed off. She looked around and realized that the two sad lightbulbs high above were turned off. Nehir was moving the rugs, and Evie breathed a sigh of relief as the pressure on her bladder lessened. Damn, did she have to think about her bladder?

"Nehir, I need the toilet." She knew the word bathroom didn't translate.

"Must wait. Must home." Evie looked over to the one and only entry to the store, and Zehra was in the process of pulling the security gate closed. Nehir, meanwhile, was shoving colorful clothing at Evie. It was a rust-colored tunic that would fall to the ground and cover her top and jeans. There was also a scarf for her to wear over her head. Neither Zehra or Nehir wore scarves, but she could see the wisdom of her wearing one for a disguise. One of the women must have gone to another stall and purchased an outfit for her while she was sleeping.

After Evie was done dressing, Nehir rushed her to the front of the shop while pushing a small rug into her hands. It was clear that she was supposed to be a late shopper.

When she went into the throng of people who were busy getting their last minute items, there was a man who stood out. He was huge, and he stood in the middle of the mall, surveying the crowd. He wasn't the one who had followed her. It made Evie shiver. This was worse than she thought. How many people were after her? Evie bowed her head and looked at Zehra and Nehir and held out her rug.

"*Teşekkür ederim.*" Evie bowed to the two of them as they exited.

She continued to thank them as they scurried down the small street, relieved to see they weren't capturing anyone's notice. Zehra linked her arm with Evie's as they made their way down the busy alley.

"We must hurry," she whispered to Evie. "People have been looking for you."

Damn! What in the hell had happened? Just as she'd thought that, they were rushing past the restrooms.

"Stop!"

"Evie, we must get to my home."

"I have to pee." It was urgent.

Zehra looked at Evie, and then grabbed the rug out of her arms. "Go. But hurry. These are bad men. We need to get you to safety. Nehir and I will wait here for you."

Evie walked slowly into the old building, taking care not to call attention to herself. She kept her head down and was grateful there was no line. She did her business and then called Blake's phone. It went to voicemail.

She called Jim next. His went to voicemail too. She texted them.

HELP. SOMEONE IS AFTER ME WITH A GUN. WILL TRY TO GET TO EMBASSY.

When she went back outside, she looked around and couldn't find either Zehra or Nehir. Instead, she saw the precious rug crumpled in the dirt.

Pain screamed up her arm as it was yanked up and backward. Her wrist was wrapped in a bone-crushing grip.

"Make a sound and your friends die." The words were said with a foul-smelling breath and an English accent, which just made the moment all the more surreal.

Evie gritted her teeth against the pain. "What do you want?"

"Do you know where the passports are?" he demanded, as he pulled her deeper into the shadow of the old building.

"I'll give you my passport. Please don't hurt the women."

Where were Zehra and Nehir? How could he kill them, if he had her?

He jerked her arm higher up her back. Evie felt the joint pop and cried out. The man clapped his hand over her mouth. "I told you not to make any noise." Tears dripped down over her nose and onto his big hand. The pain in her shoulder was excruciating.

"I don't want your passport. I want *the* passports."

He moved his hand so she could answer.

"I don't know what you're talking about," she whimpered.

"Fine, I'll use you to make the others give me what I want."

What was he talking about?

He pulled on her arm even more. The pain was an oily smear, she was going to throw up. Or pass out. "I won't hesitate to kill those two women if you scream. Do you understand me?"

Please, God, say that she was right, and he didn't have Nehir and Zehra.

"Walk with me."

He took a step forward.

No!

Evie dug in her heels. The moment she left the bazaar with him, she was a dead woman.

Flecks of oregano seasoned lamb sprayed on her, as he hissed, "Fine, we'll do this the hard way."

He shoved her arm up even higher. Waves of pain crashed through her brain, flickers of flame burned her eyeballs, then everything went black.

Chapter Three

Three Days Later – San Diego, California USA

It seemed odd to be sitting in a bar like this without cigarette smoke. Maybe he should have gone down to Tijuana. He looked at the amber liquid in his glass. The twenty-year-old Irish whiskey wouldn't get the job done, not at the glacial rate he was drinking it. What was the point? Nothing would make him feel better but time.

He stared at his phone. The call he had earlier was still messing with his head. Discovering that NiNi's death was a random act of violence, and not a hit by the Deuces gang, was unbelievable. Even more remarkable was Sam's conviction that Aiden was well and truly off the Deuces' radar.

He twirled the glass and watched the whiskey swirl. He needed to calm his thinking. Instead, it was spinning out of control. Nothing had gone right since he received the phone call about NiNi's death when he was in Tennessee three months ago. At the time, everybody in Chicago had thought that it had been one of the Deuce's soldiers who had taken her out. Sam, his dad's old partner, had been ready to take down every gang member. It was his brothers in blue and his kids who had kept him sane.

So, while Sam had gone off the deep end in Chicago, Aiden had followed in his footsteps down in Tennessee. He was sure that damn near twenty years later, the Deuces had killed the woman who had been like a second mother to him. And that meant that soon they would be after him and whomever he held dear. What were the odds? Twenty-one years after having called down the wrath of those fuckers he'd found Eva Avery, but in order to keep her safe, he had to throw her away.

He swallowed the alcohol and appreciated the burn.

It was one in the morning. He'd been nursing his second drink for three hours. The waitress knew him. He came in maybe once a month when his missions allowed it. He tipped well, so she didn't care that he took up valuable real estate for hours, nursing one or two drinks.

Aiden watched as she headed toward him.

"Another?"

He gave a brief shake of his head.

"I'll leave you to it then." She smiled and sashayed to another table, leaving him at his back booth.

He fingered his phone. It'd been eight hours since Sam had called.

Sam Chang had been adamant about the fact that he'd been wrong when he'd called him three months earlier. NiNi's death had nothing to do with old vendettas.

Aiden carefully set down the glass, when everything in him wanted to hurl it across the bar. Fuck! He'd destroyed Evie's trust, sure that his past was back, and that any woman who meant something to him would end up dead.

He shut his eyes and breathed deeply. He needed to get a grip on his emotions. Peace. He had worked hard for it. When action was required, he reacted. Precisely. Effectively. Deadly. But first, he needed to collect his calm. It was how he always accomplished things. If it was possible to win, he won. This would be no different. He looked at the unbroken glass and nodded.

So now, once again, he would proceed with calm. He would plan. He would execute.

The hair on the back of his neck prickled, and he looked at the door. He wasn't surprised to see one of his oldest friends walk in. He hadn't seen Gray Tyler in two months. Gray led his old SEAL team, Black Dawn. He must have heard about the goat fuck of a mission that he had just come off of. Little did the man know, the real goat fuck had happened three months ago.

Gray didn't even look around the shadowy bar. His eyes lasered to the back booth where Aiden sat, and he headed to him.

The man slipped into the opposite chair. Kimmie was at his shoulder in an instant.

"Duvel," Gray said, ordering his beer.

"Gotchya." She disappeared.

"I heard," Gray said. "Talked to Mason. The man was basically dead when you arrived at the compound."

Aiden just stared at his friend. It was easier to let the man think that the reason he was at the bar was due to the mission.

"That's not the way I see it."

"You wouldn't," Gray sighed.

"You here to give me a pep talk?"

"Just here for a beer." Kimmie slid a bottle and glass in front of Gray and walked off. "How much does that cost you?" Gray motioned to the short glass in front of Aiden.

"If you have to ask, you can't afford it."

Gray chuckled as he poured his beer into the glass. "I forgot you come from money."

"Don't forget the criminal element that comes with it," Aiden said wryly.

"Now that I don't forget. A couple of those stories are burned into my memory."

Thinking about his rich uncle down in the Yucatan peninsula always made Aiden smile. The man had been a major player in his younger days. Hell, even now his reach extended all the way to Veracruz, Mexico. It was only because his late father, the Irish cop from Chicago, was totally in love with his wife, that he could cope with her nefarious family.

"You used to think I made that stuff up," Aiden reminded his former lieutenant.

"Not after Leonard Canul came to visit. That man is a trip and a half."

"He wanted to make sure Beth and Jack were doing okay," Aiden said, referring to his current teammate's fiancée.

"That was one hell of an ordeal she went through."

"You wouldn't guess it looking at her, but she kicked ass."

"I heard that too. But, yeah, she seems like a shy thing compared to her sister Lydia."

Aiden just shook his head. The women of Midnight Delta were pretty amazing.

Then he thought about Evie again.

"What?" Gray asked.

"Nothing."

"That's more than a nothing face."

Aiden tilted his head. "Don't push."

Gray took a long sip of his beer. "The last time I saw you, you were in bad space too, what the hell is up?"

Aiden just stared at Gray, not saying anything.

"If you don't tell me, I'm going to guess, and you won't be happy."

"Leave it alone," Aiden clipped out.

"It's a woman."

"In the entire eight years have you known me, has it ever been a woman?" Aiden asked.

"Nope. Still is, though."

Aiden sighed. "How'd you guess?"

"One, I know you. Two, you hook up with Midnight Delta, you somehow end up with women issues. Everybody on base is talking about how they're like the Match.com of SEAL teams."

Aiden shook his head and laughed. It was so true. Then he gave Gray a sly look. "So, when are you going to do a mission with us? Aren't you tired of being alone?"

"We weren't talking about me, O'Malley, we were talking about you sipping fifty dollar drinks. Anyway, I have a team of my own to run, and your ass is going to be back to it in two more months."

Aiden thought about his old teammates and smiled. He missed them, especially Griff and Dexter, but then again, he really liked his new teammates, even Drake Avery. If he hadn't fucked up with his sister, they'd be friends.

"Again, you're looking like your dog died."

"I am not." Aiden knew his expression hadn't changed. After he was sixteen, he'd learned how to mask everything if he chose to, so he was surprised by Gray's comment.

"Face it, I'm your best friend, I've been studying you for years. So, what's her name?"

"Evie," Aiden admitted reluctantly.

"Is she the one?"

Aiden didn't answer.

"What the hell is your problem? If she's the one, why not go after her?"

He didn't respond.

"Aiden?"

"I screwed up. I thought I was doing the right thing. But I hurt her."

"Apologize."

"It's not that easy. You don't know her."

"Women love it when men admit they're wrong."

"Evie is Drake Avery's sister."

"Avery's sister?" Gray gave him an incredulous look. "Yeah, this is going to require more than an apology." He laughed. Then he sobered. "You never answered my question. Is she the one?"

"I didn't give us a chance."

"That's a damn shame. Are you going to her?"

"I need to think about it. I want to make sure I have a game plan."

"Jesus, O'Malley, it's simple. Apologize and start over."

"I want to make sure I don't end up hurting her again."

Chapter Four

Same Day – Somewhere in Turkey

"Wake up!" It was the man with the English accent. He was back. After the first day, she'd been left alone in the dank little room, waiting, and now he was back. The first night she'd shoved her shoulder back into its socket and passed out from the pain. Eventually, she awoke and made friends with the cement floor. Finally, she crawled onto the dirty mattress in the corner of what amounted to her cell. She used the tunic to rest her head on.

When she'd woken the following day, she'd wondered what had happened to Zehra and Nehir. Hopefully, her gut had been right, and they had never been in the asshole's clutches. Hopefully, they knew somebody to contact for help. Then there were Blake and Jim. They would be looking for her since she had called and texted them.

Help had to be coming soon.

"I said wake up!"

As soon as her brain swirled to consciousness, her first panicked thought was to ascertain whether she had her clothes on.

That was always where her attention went first when she woke up. She gave an imperceptible sigh of relief that she was still clothed, then cracked open an eyelid. As soon as she saw the man was holding a bucket, she jerked upwards. There was no way she wanted to be doused with water and left in this damn cell.

He held up her cell phone. "It's time to make another movie."

They'd done that when they first threw her in the dirty little room. He'd made her tell Jim and Blake that she was being held captive and they had one week to deliver the passports or she would die.

She believed him.

But what fucking passports was he talking about?!

"Sure, I'll make another movie, if you'll tell me what passports you're talking about," Evie said.

"Still playing dumb, are you?"

"You can say I'm playing or you can just call me dumb. I don't care which. Just explain to me why I'm lying on this dirty floor with the threat of death hanging over my head."

"Your lovers are working with Nathan Alderman and have eighty blank South American passports that I've paid for. I want what's mine."

Evie looked at the man incredulously. First, the fact that the committed gay couple could be her lovers was crazy town, then the idea that they would traffic in something as dangerous as blank passports, was crazy town squared.

Holy shit on a cracker. No wonder she was lying on hard cement and pissing in a bucket.

"You're wrong," she finally croaked out.

"I'm not wrong. It's time to up the incentive for them to give me back my property."

He went back to the door of the cell and threw it open. He

muttered in Turkish and in walked another man. The man who spoke in English held up her phone. She recognized the pink covering.

"Action!"

The second man grabbed her by the hair, lifted her off the ground and hit her across the face.

Evie grunted in pain.

He hit her again. This time she cried out.

The third time he punched her, she screamed.

Evie didn't know when she started to cry.

She reached out for a happy moment to cling to and found herself back in Tennessee.

He continued to hit her until she finally passed out.

* * *

Flashback - Three Months Ago

He was beautiful. All that luscious blond hair and blue eyes. Come to find out he was half Mexican and half Irish. What a gorgeous combination. Then the way his eyes sparkled when he looked at her. She was in heaven. Not that she ever intended to let him know that.

"You're our guard dog?"

"Evie, be nice," her baby sister, Piper, said. "This is Aiden. He's staying with us. He's going to help me with my homework."

"I'm going to go make dinner." Evie stomped past Aiden and Piper in the great room and headed for the kitchen. She needed to take a breather before she drooled on the carpet. God, he was like something out of the romance novels she read.

Her head in the refrigerator, she took stock of what was

available to make a meal. She grabbed the first thing that looked promising.

"Hey, what's your problem?"

Evie jumped damn near four feet and dropped the roast she'd been holding. She whirled around.

"What in the hell are you doing sneaking up on me?" She stared up and up and up so that she could face the man who must be a foot and a half taller than she was.

He squatted and picked up the roast, and stayed there so they were nose to nose.

"What's your problem, little girl?"

"Stud muffin, I'm not your little girl. We have Piper and my niece, Bella, to take that role. I'm the one who will poison your food, put nettles in your bed, and put Nair in your shampoo if you mess with me."

The man's eyes lit up, then he threw back his head and laughed.

"How old are you? Five?"

"I'm seventeen, old man. Are you feeling like a perv?" she taunted.

He chuckled again. "Are you twenty-six yet?"

Shit, how did he know how old she was. Her eyes narrowed. "Have you been checking up on my family?"

"Like you said, I'm the guard dog. Gotta know what I'm guarding, Evalyn."

"Call me Eva." He stood up and handed her the roast. "You cook?"

"Well duh."

"I promised Piper we'd watch a movie after her homework was done, do you want to join us?"

She worked hard to keep her eyes on his face, and not let

them drift to those wide shoulders that were showcased in the blue turtleneck that matched his eyes.

"You're not letting her decide what to watch, are you?"

"Sure, why not?"

"It'll be sappy," Evie noted.

"I can do sappy." He grinned.

Damn, he had a dimple.

Evie felt her girl parts tingle. She could do sappy too, she just didn't tell many people that. Okay, she didn't tell anyone. She always pretended she only did shoot-em-ups.

"Let me get dinner started."

"Need some help?" Aiden asked.

"Do you know how to cook?"

"Do I look like I've gone hungry in the last few years?"

She lost the fight and took in the breadth of the man's shoulders. His eyes gleamed. He noted her perusal. Her cheeks pinkened.

"You don't look like you've missed a meal. Okay, we're having pot roast, mashed potatoes, gravy, green beans, creamed corn, and peach cobbler for dessert. Think you can help with all of that?"

"Lady, I'm your slave."

If only he'd said love slave.

* * *

Next Day – San Diego, California

Mason gave him a considering look.

"You've got plenty of leave available, but you and I know that it's not going to help. Now, if you were running to something, instead of away..." Mason let his words hang in the air.

"I'm not running away from anything. I'm taking some time away to think."

Mason raised his eyebrow. Finally, he said, "I'll approve it."

Aiden's head whipped around at the sound of Mason's office door slamming open. Drake stormed into the office and took all of the oxygen out of the room.

"Mase, I've got to leave now."

"Karen?" he and Mason asked simultaneously. They both knew that Drake's fiancée was five months pregnant.

"She's fine." Drake waved his hand. "It's Evie. She's missing."

Before Aiden could say a word, Drake continued. "She went to Italy and Greece a couple of weeks ago. Apparently, she's been missing for the last few days. She hasn't checked in with Trenda like she's been doing every day."

Aiden stood up and shot Drake an icy glare. "Just what the hell do you mean your little sister went to Europe? She's never been out of the state of Tennessee." Aiden was quickly processing the information. Missing. Europe. Bloody hell! As much as he tried to keep calm, all he could think was that Eva Lavender's ass should be firmly planted in Tennessee with the rest of her eighty sisters.

Drake's palm shot out, shutting down his question. "I wasn't talking to you, O'Malley."

Well, there went the three months of faking it in front of Mason.

Drake turned toward their commander. "Mason, she's not in Greece anymore. Six days ago, they went to Turkey."

"Who's they?" Mason asked.

"Jim and Blake," Drake answered.

"What was she doing in Turkey with her two bosses?" Aiden demanded. He immediately went through what he knew about the two men. Jim was a former Army Ranger and Blake a former Marine. They were lovers. They owned the small, exclusive hotel where Evie worked.

"According to Trenda, they took her along on vacation. Everybody knew that she was in bad space because of you, and they took pity on her." Drake glared at Aiden.

"So, have you gotten in touch with either of them?" Aiden asked.

"Don't ask stupid questions." Drake glared at him. "Of course, I've tried to get ahold of them. Blake talked to Trenda yesterday. He said not to worry about Evie. She was indisposed and that she would call tomorrow. Which is today. When she didn't call, Trenda tried to get ahold of Blake and Jim, but neither of them is answering. That's when she called me."

"She should have called you the first day that Evie didn't check in with her," Aiden said.

"Don't you get on Trenda's case," Drake growled, but he was rubbing the back of his neck. It was clear that he agreed with Aiden. He turned to look at Mason. "Mase, I need to leave now. Can you and Sophia look in on Karen and Piper?"

"You've got it. Are you going to Turkey?" Mason asked.

"Before I head half-cocked to Turkey, I'm going to Tennessee and do a quick recon of Blake and Jim's office at their home and hotel."

"I'm going with you," Aiden said.

Drake turned on him. "I wasn't fucking talking to you, O'Malley. This is family business, so stay the hell out of it!"

"Can it, Avery," Mason said quietly. Drake went silent, his entire focus on Mason. "Is there anything else to tell?"

Drake breathed in through his nose.

"I didn't even know that Evie had left the country. For fuck's sake, if she wanted to take a vacation, why didn't she start with California? Trenda said that Blake and Jim arranged for her passport to be fast-tracked so she could go to Italy and Greece with them. Then they suddenly decided to go Turkey."

"Evie had been calling Trenda every day. She had some kind of international calling plan. That's all I've got. I need to get a flight to Tennessee."

Mason nodded.

"You've just gained yourself some company," Aiden said.

"Fuck that noise." Drake didn't even look at him.

"I'm going to Tennessee, and then to Turkey, and then to wherever else it might lead." They all knew that Turkey butted up to Syria and Iraq. God knew what in the hell mess Blake and Jim had gotten into.

"I can't hear this. All I can hear is that you are going to Tennessee. But if you need back-up, let me know." Mason said to Drake.

There it was. Once again, Mason Gault proved himself as a friend and a commander. He'd go into the fire with his men just like Gray. He'd fight to the death for either man.

"Thanks, man. But I need to know you have my back with Karen, Piper, and the baby. I need you here in San Diego taking care of them."

"They'll be taken care of." Aiden heard the subtext. There were the five women of Midnight Delta who would circle the wagons and take care of Drake's woman and youngest sister. Meanwhile, the men of Midnight Delta would be on call to run to the ends of the Earth and help Drake find his other sister.

"I'm going with you, Drake. When are we leaving?"

"Are you for real? I don't want you within a thousand miles of this. We work together, that's it."

Aiden chuckled. "Stop sounding like a girl. Hell, not even Evie sounds as whiny as you do."

"You motherfucker. She cried. You made my little sister cry."

"That's between me and her. Her safety is all I care about. Don't be a hotheaded asshole who turns down help. We're out of here yesterday." He turned to Mason. "My leave starts now. Sounds like I have something I'm running to."

"Sounds like," Mason agreed grimly.

* * *

As soon as they rounded the corner in the hallway, Drake turned on him. "We're taking this outside."

"You dumb son-of-a-bitch. We're taking this off-base. As a matter of fact, it'll be decided in Tennessee."

"You're crazy if you think you're going."

Aiden looked at Drake. They were damn near the same size, so it'd be close. They might actually end up killing one another.

"We're on the same side," Aiden said evenly.

"I'm on Evie's side. You fucked her over. I don't know what happened. Hell, I don't want to know what happened. But my ball-busting sister ended up crying. The last thing I want is you within a hundred miles of her. *Capisce*?"

"Not *capisce*. I admit I fucked up. I'm going to fix it. In the meantime, Evie needs help. I'm going whether you approve or not."

"You'll find the doors closed."

"Not when I say I'm sorry and I'm there to help. Not one of your sisters will turn down an iota of help. They have more sense than you do."

Drake stared at him.

"They'll back Evie," Drake said decisively.

"Why are we standing here? Don't we have a plane to catch?"

Drake turned and walked down the hall, leaving Aiden to stare after him. Jesus, the man was stubborn.

Chapter Five

Same Day – Somewhere in Turkey

"You're lucky. It seems that your friends are going to come through for you."

Evie could only hear every other word. Something about being lucky and her friends? Where was she? She was cold. Something tasted coppery.

"I need you to open your eyes and talk."

Pain streaked through her scalp.

"Woman, are you listening to me? Open your eyes!"

The evil man's face swam in front of her. She had always liked shows like Downton Abbey, now the English accent was going to make her throw up.

"Good, now say something."

Evie swallowed and tasted blood. Finally, she was able to form a word.

"Something," she gasped out.

The man laughed. "You have spirit. I like that."

She didn't want him to like her. She wanted him dead. She spat out the blood, gratified when it hit him in the face. He slapped her.

"Bitch, don't make me *really* hurt you. Now, it's time to make another video. Your friends are worried about you. If you do what I ask, I'll get you some water and food."

She didn't want anything from him, but if she was going to survive this horror, she needed food and water.

"What do you want?" she asked.

"Sit up against the wall." He propped her up against the wall. It was hard to stay upright, but she managed. He pointed her phone in her direction. He must have a charger, Evie thought. She rolled her eyes. What a weird thing to think of now. How was he using it? Oh, yeah, she'd given him the passcode the first day when he kept yanking on her arm.

"Tell Richards that you're okay."

"I'm okay," she croaked out.

"Say more than that," he commanded.

She looked at the man holding the phone in confusion. What else was there to say? Then she realized what she wanted to say.

"Tell my family I love them. Please, Blake. Tell my sisters and Drake that I love them." Evie paused. "Tell Aiden I was thinking about him, too."

"That'll do."

The man turned around and left the room.

Evie slipped down the wall and fell sideways onto the dirty mattress. She coughed out a laugh. How lame was that? *Tell Aiden I was thinking about him.*

A tear dripped down her face. No matter how angry, how hurt, how everything, she was always thinking about Aiden

O'Malley. That was why she was halfway around the world in the first place.

She closed her eyes and slipped back to Tennessee.

* * *

Flashback, Tennessee, Three Months Ago

She glared at Aiden.

"This is my bedroom. Did you get lost, Kitten?"

"Did you just call me Kitten?"

He grinned at her.

"Oh my fucking God, you did. Are you out of your ever-loving mind?"

She stormed across the room to where he was putting his clothes into a drawer, and stared up at him. He looked down at her, his eyes dancing.

"It seemed more politically correct than hell cat, but if you would prefer…"

"I didn't come up here for you to call me dumbass names, I came up here to demand that you follow my brother. He shouldn't go out on his own. You should be watching his back."

"No," Aiden said calmly. "I'm right where I need to be."

"Are you a coward?" Evie taunted.

"You just don't back down, do you?" He chuckled

The man didn't seem bothered in the slightest by her comment. Damn, she really thought that calling a Navy SEAL chicken would get under his skin.

"I need you to get out there and catch up with Drake. He's walking into a trap!"

"There isn't a chance in hell that your brother needs my help. He is more than capable of handling things on his own.

What's more, I need to play my position. I'm responsible for protecting you, Karen, your sisters, and your niece. I take that responsibility very seriously." His blue eyes gleamed.

"This place is a fortress. We're on lockdown. Give me a weapon, and we're good." Evie thought about her big brother, and it was killing her. She hadn't seen him in over a decade. The idea that he might end up dead was too much for her to handle. Aiden had to go and help him.

He must have seen her anguish.

"Kitten, it's going to be alright."

"No, it's not. Please, go, before it's too late."

"There is no one I would trust more than your brother. He's got this."

Ah God, she could feel tears beginning to form. Aiden put one hand gently on her shoulder, and his other hand brushed back her hair. "Eva, I have to stay here. I need to make sure all of you are safe. Drake couldn't do what he needs to if he didn't know that you were taken care of."

"Please, Aiden," she begged. "I can't lose him."

"You won't. You have to believe me. You don't know him like I do. He's a legend." Aiden gave her a half grin. "But I'll deny it if you ever tell him I said it."

Evie felt the knot in her belly begin to dissolve as she looked up into Aiden's blue eyes.

"Anyway, he's too much like you to ever let anything happen to him."

"Huh?"

"Eva, you have no fear, you came at me today like a virago. I thought you were going to take my head off with that damn mop."

Her lips twisted. "Yeah, sure."

"Seriously, you actually took me by surprise. I wasn't expecting that swing of yours. I wouldn't kid you."

"You were able to sidestep it easily enough," she said wryly.

"For God's sake, I would hope so. It still surprised me." His thumb brushed her cheek. "Tell me, how often have you had to defend yourself like that?"

She couldn't help the betraying flinch, and the damned perceptive man caught it. "Tell me," he persisted.

"Not often," she said softly.

"Tell me," he repeated.

"Sometimes guys get the wrong idea when they're too close to a bed, and there's a woman close. I remind them real quick what maid service does and doesn't include." *Please, let him think that was the worst.*

Evie watched Aiden's features turn to granite. "How badly have you been hurt?" he asked quietly.

"Jim and Blake are always a scream away," she said side-stepping his question.

His expression darkened.

"Except for today. Jim and Blake are in Australia. There was nobody to scream for, now was there?" he bit out. "Here you are bitching about your brother with no backup, and you were out there with your ass flying in the wind, never mind the normal losers, but you have a bunch of convicts gunning for your family, and you're just running around like there isn't a worry in the world. Jesus, woman, you have no sense!"

Damn, when he put it like that…

"Ah, the light dawns," he growled.

She jerked out of his hold. She hated that he was right.

"Eva-"

She whirled back to stare at him. "You should stop calling me that. Everybody else is calling me Evie these days." She should have never told him to call her Eva. It made her feel special.

"You introduced yourself to me as Eva. It's a beautiful name, for a beautiful woman."

Gah! She was five feet nothing and pretty at best, while he was a walking Greek god.

"Don't change the subject, Kitten. We aren't done talking about the foolish chances you took today."

"Fine! I was out of line, is that what you want to hear?"

"I want to hear you promise not to do it again."

"Fine! I won't do it again."

And she wouldn't. He was right, damn him. She'd had her head up her ass. All she'd thought about was her responsibilities at the hotel, not the fact that it was possible she was in danger, and it would divert resources from taking care of Piper. Fuck! Fuckity-fuck. She'd totally screwed up.

"You're absolutely right. I was a dumbass." She sighed.

Aiden's blond eyebrows rose, and then he grinned. He walked the two steps over to her, and swept her into a hug. She pushed against his chest.

"What's your deal?" she demanded.

"I love how you are so up front. You just tell it like it is, don't you? There are no games where you're concerned. You get pissed off, you're in my face. When you're worried about your brother, you're not afraid to show your love and concern. And finally, you're not afraid to admit when you're wrong. You're quite a woman, Eva Lavender."

She scowled up at him.

"You don't have to use my middle name."

"What, you don't like it? How about Kitten?"

She rolled her eyes.

He gave her a breathtaking smile.

"I think I'm going to stick with Kitten." Then he bent close and whispered in her ear. "You and I will know it really means hell cat."

* * *

Same Day - Tennessee

Drake's sister, Trenda, and her three-and-a-half-year-old daughter Bella were waiting for them at baggage claim.

"Unca Dwake!" Bella called out as she ran towards him.

For the first time since Aiden had seen him in Mason's office, he saw Drake smile. He swept his niece high into the air. She giggled.

"Hi, Pumpkin. How's my favorite girl?"

"You came. I has a unicorn. Mommy has her. You wanna see?"

"I would love to." Drake smiled.

Suddenly the little girl caught sight of Aiden.

"Mister O-Man?" Aiden grinned, tickled that little Bella remembered him.

"Hi, Bella."

The girl gave him a sweet smile, and her mother grabbed her out of Drake's arms and cuddled her close to her chest, and scowled at him. Her expression was so reminiscent of Evie it made his heart clench. She turned to Drake.

"What is he doing here?" she hissed.

Drake sighed. "I couldn't scrape him off."

"You should have tried harder."

"He's going with me to Turkey. An extra set of eyes and hands will be welcome."

Aiden kept his expression neutral. That was the first time Drake had said anything positive, and he wasn't going to ruin it.

"Just make sure that if anyone is in the line of fire, it's him, and not you, and I'll be happy." Trenda glared at him again, and Aiden laughed. God, he loved these Avery sisters. They were bloodthirsty, and they didn't hold back.

"Don't you dare laugh at me," she railed at him in a stage whisper, so that Bella wasn't disturbed. It didn't work.

"What's funny, Mommy?"

"Your Momma's funny. She's just like your Aunt Evie," Aiden answered. It was the absolute wrong thing to say. Bella's lip trembled. She turned her head to her mother and placed both hands on her face and smooshed her cheeks.

"Where's Auntie Evie? I want Auntie Evie, Mommy." Then she promptly burst into tears.

Trenda tenderly grabbed her little girl's hand and kissed her palm. "Aunt Evie will be home soon, Baby." Trenda shot Aiden a dirty look.

"You're right, she will be," Aiden said.

"Damn straight," Drake said at the same time. He looked at his niece who was still sniffling.

"I swore, don't I owe you some money?" he asked. The little girl just stared at him. "Don't you remember our game, Peanut?" he prompted.

"She's too upset." Trenda sighed.

"A deal is a deal." He pulled out his wallet and extracted a dollar. "Here you go, kid."

Bella bit her lip, then offered him a wan smile. "You said a bad word."

"I did. So you earn a dollar."

"You really shouldn't encourage her, Drake," Trenda cautioned her brother. "But I'm glad you did."

Drake reached out and cupped the back of her sister's neck. He touched his forehead to hers. "We've got this. Take us to the hotel. We want to go through Blake and Jim's office. Have you been able to get ahold of them while we were in the air?" he asked quietly.

"No," she whispered. "Their voicemail is full. I keep texting them to call me. I also left your phone number on the texts so they might get ahold of you."

"Good idea, Baby." He smiled at Trenda. "We'll get her. I promise."

Bella patted her uncle's face as she relaxed between two of her favorite people. It was a touching scene.

* * *

When they got to the small hotel right outside Jasper Creek, Aiden allowed Drake to take charge while Trenda looked on.

"You go grab their quarters, I'm going to go through their office."

"How good are you with computers?" Aiden asked.

"Fair. Clint's our computer expert, but I have him on tap. He said that if I set up a connection, he can go through everything with a fine-tooth comb," Drake assured Aiden. He nodded. Aiden knew that Clint would find anything that could be of possible use on the men's computer system.

"Sounds like a plan."

Aiden helped himself to the keys he needed and made his way to the men's room, bypassing painters in the hallway. He wasn't surprised to find that the two military men's suite was neat as a pin. It looked as if they had combined two suites into one large set of rooms for themselves. There was a master bedroom, a living room, small kitchen and dining room. Aiden did a thorough investigation of their entire living quarters. The only things of interest were the photographs of friends and family. Aiden had to believe that everything relevant was kept in their office.

Evie's room was next. He stepped around boxes containing new light fixtures on his way down the hall. When he opened the door to her rooms, he was stunned. It was like a cyclone had hit the living room. For a moment, he thought that somebody had broken in and searched her space, but then he realized that it was upended sacks from various stores, and opened packaging that littered the floor. Evie must have packed everything at the last minute. *What the hell?* This was an absolute mess.

He picked his way through the disarray on the floor and made his way to the bedroom, and found an even worse mess. Every single drawer was open, and it looked like her entire wardrobe was piled on her bed. Had she even packed one thing? His eyes caught a bikini that was haphazardly discarded on the top of the pile. It was bright yellow and still had the tags on it. He felt a profound sense of relief that it had hit the reject pile, and she hadn't been wearing it on the beaches in Greece.

Focus, O'Malley!

Shit, when he thought about Evie Avery, he thought of jeans and flannel shirts, he never thought about bikinis and those flowy dresses that he saw on her bed. He wasn't sure he liked this. And he sure as hell didn't like the fact that men other than him would be seeing her in that type of wardrobe. Turning to look in her drawers, he smiled when he saw nothing but serviceable cotton bras and panties, but then he frowned. If there was a bikini and two discarded summer dresses on the bed, chances were there had been lacy lingerie that had been purchased and packed.

He needed to start looking to see if anything might give them an indication of what had happened to her. Looking at her wardrobe was not helping. He moved to the small desk in the corner of her room. At least that was tidy.

His phone vibrated.

"O'Malley," he answered.

"Get back here. Clint found something," Drake said. Then he hung up.

Chapter Six

"Where's Trenda?" Aiden asked.

"I waited to call you until she went to the kitchen to get something for Bella to eat."

That didn't sound good.

"Hit me," Aiden said.

"We've got three emails from the same guy." Drake handed him a printout. Aiden scanned it.

"Did Clint say who this joker is?" Aiden asked, as he threw the paper onto the desk. He'd read it. The third email was begging Jim to come to Turkey and bail him out of a jam, and bring him a shit ton of money.

"Old Army Ranger buddy of Jim's."

"He wanted thirty thousand dollars out of the blue? Do these guys have that kind of money laying around?"

"According to Clint, yeah. Jim arranged for a transfer of funds to a bank in Turkey."

Aiden's gut clenched. "Please, God, don't tell me he took the money out in cash."

Drake stared at him.

"Goddammit," Aiden whispered harshly. "Just how close were Jim and this guy?"

"Nathan was a hero. He saved their entire unit. When he left the Army, he did some time as a mercenary, but they kicked him out for drugs. Since then, he's been a fuck-up. Clint managed to pull up all the correspondence between Nathan and Jim. They've kept in touch for years, but this is the first time he's asked for help. He must have kept tabs on Jim, and known he was in Europe and decided to make a play." Drake sounded pissed and worried at the same time.

"How stupid is Jim?" Aiden asked in disbelief. Pulling that large of an amount of cash out of a bank in Turkey would have raised all kinds of red flags. He would have caught the eye of the Turkish government, besides the fact that he would be involved with God-knew-what kind of criminals.

"Stupid," Drake said, pounding his fist on the desk. "Clint's doing a deep background check on Nathan Alderman. By the time we get to Turkey, he should have his great-grandparents' middle names, as well his underwear size."

"I want Dexter working on this," Aiden said, as he pulled out his phone.

Drake's mouth dropped open. "What the hell are you talking about?" he roared. "Clint and Lydia will have this wrapped up tighter than a tick," he said, referring to Clint's fiancée. Aiden didn't have time for the fight. He pressed Dex's number, and walked out of the office into the hall.

"I heard. Whatever you need, I'm here for you." Aiden relaxed at the sound of his friend's deep voice. Dexter Evans was more than just the resident tech guru on the Black Dawn SEAL team. Years ago, they'd realized they came from similar backgrounds. Dex's dad was a cop who had been gunned down in Seattle, and Dex had arranged for revenge.

Dex and Aiden understood one another at a soul level.

"I need you to go deep, and I don't care what laws you have to break or who you have to hack."

"Gray said your woman has been taken."

Aiden paused, gripping the bridge of his nose between his fingers. "I was stupid Dex, I threw away my shot because of crap from my past. I don't know if she is my woman, but I *do* know she's in a world of trouble."

"Then we get her out of trouble, and you grovel. It's that simple."

Aiden barked out a laugh. God, he loved this man. "Sure it is. You don't know Evie."

"Groveling works wonders. Chocolate, diamonds, and orgasms also need to be on the agenda, and you'll be fine."

Aiden felt his heart lighten. "Okay, here's what you need to know," he started.

"No need. I'll just tap into Clint's computer."

Aiden raised his eyebrow. "It can't possibly be that easy. His shit is tight."

"Nah, that last joint mission we went on, he thought he was being sneaky when he tapped into my system. I let him do it because I knew that I could use it to backdoor into his."

"He did that to you? That's totally out of line." Aiden's blood began to boil.

"Relax. I'd been flirting pretty hard with Lydia. I set it up."

"You are one twisted bastard." Aiden pictured Clint's face when Dexter started hitting on his woman. He would have pushed back a little, but he was the type of man who would have wanted to get even.

"So give me five minutes to get up to speed, another twenty to do all of the illegal shit that Clint might have steered away from. But I've got to tell you, for Drake's sister, I don't think he would have let anything stop him from getting information."

"I know." Aiden sighed. "But, here's the deal. I need you to get in touch with my uncle. That will open up an abundance of information from the criminal element. He'll talk to you, he won't talk to Clint."

"Gotchya. Anything else?"

"As soon as it makes sense, pool your resources. No point in having you, Clint, and Lydia working at odds."

"I'll call him after I talk to your uncle."

Aiden went back into the office. Drake looked up and punched a button on his phone. "I just put you on speaker, Mason."

"Aiden, we don't need people tripping over their dicks. Drake is right, let Clint handle this."

Aiden winced. He knew Mason was angry if he was talking like that. He was normally much calmer.

"Dex is calling my Uncle Leonard right now. Even though he's in Mexico, his network of friends and resources is vast. After he loops in with Uncle, he'll be calling your people."

"Goddammit, O'Malley, it isn't a matter of us and them. We're all SEALs. You need to cut that out right now." There was a pause, and Aiden could hear Mason's wheels turning. "Tell me how in the hell does Dexter know enough information to talk intelligently to your uncle, if he hasn't already talked to Clint or Lydia?" Before Aiden could open his mouth, Drake was starting to swear.

"Shut it, Avery," Mason shouted over the phone. "O'Malley, is Dexter surveilling my team members?"

"I think you'll find that the surveillance goes both ways, Lieutenant," Aiden said carefully.

"Dammit." The phone went dead. Aiden knew Mason was calling Clint.

"Black Dawn has eyes and ears on Midnight Delta?" Drake asked menacingly.

"Oh for fuck's sake. I think you, Mason, and I are looking at it totally different than the computer dweebs. They look at it as some kind of damn game. I think they have some kind of weird scoreboard, and they probably buy each other drinks at some bar we're not invited to. Mellow the fuck out, Drake. Dex and Clint are good, and…" He looked down at the watch on his wrist. "In three more minutes, they'll be working together on this project to help us figure out where Evie is."

"Still doesn't make it right that your guy is fucking with my guy."

"Drake, we're back," Trenda called out a warning as she rounded the corner. Obviously, she'd heard her big brother's rant.

He glared one last time at Aiden before he smiled at his sister and niece.

Trenda handed off her squirming daughter to a glowering Drake, and he was immediately soothed. "You're going to make a good Daddy." Bella settled in his arms, and Trenda looked between the two men. "What have you found out?"

"There is an old friend of Jim's who asked him to go to Turkey and give him some money,," Drake answered.

"How much money?"

"Thirty thousand dollars," Aiden told her. "Have you ever heard him talk about a guy named Nathan Alderman?"

Trenda shook her head. "I wouldn't know I don't hang out with Evie and the guys that much. This Nathan guy would have to be a heck of a friend. Was he an Army buddy?"

"How'd you know?" Aiden questioned.

"It's the only thing that makes sense. Outside of each other and their families, the only people who are close to them, are Evie and their former military buddies."

"We have some of our computer folks checking into him. They'll find out everything about him," Drake assured his sister.

Aiden's phone rang. It was Dexter, and he put it on speaker. "Keep it clean, we have women and children listening to you," Aiden warned.

"Hi, all y'all. I'm Dexter." Bella giggled at the man's exaggerated Southern accent.

"Cut the comedy, and tell us what you know," Drake demanded.

"Hold on, I'm connecting Clint and Lydia."

There was a pause, and then Clint's disgruntled voice came on the line. "Archer here."

"What do you have?"

"I think I need to take Bella back to the kitchen," Trenda said, reaching for her daughter.

Drake nodded and handed over the little girl.

As soon as they were out of the office, Aiden spoke into the phone. "It's clear to talk."

"Nathan's gotten involved with some bad guys," Dexter said. "I mean some *really* bad guys. The ones who sell their services to terrorists."

"Has *he* crossed that line?" Aiden asked.

"Not yet, but he's been doing them a lot of favors. He's a gambler and a bad one. Last year he had to sell his house in Dallas to pay off his debts, and it's just gotten worse."

"So that's why he's making deals with terrorists. Do we know why he's in Turkey?"

"The outfit he's working with is RLI. It stands for Red Line International. They're former fuck-ups from Special Forces.

Most of them have been dishonorably discharged, but that doesn't stop them from making up outrageous resumes. Hell, one of them says he's a retired lieutenant general. Anyway, they're being hired right and left, and besides offering their expertise, they're brokering arms deals. But there is a rumor that they have some blank South American passports to sell."

"Holy God," Aiden breathed. "Those are worth their weight in gold. Where would they have gotten their hands on those?"

"One of these assholes was stationed in Baghdad. That's where thousands of the passports supposedly went missing. He could have gotten his hands on some, or he knows somebody who has some," Dex answered.

"Do you think they would trust Nathan with brokering the passport deal?" Drake asked.

"Right now these guys are in Africa on a job. I think they needed someone and Nathan was available. But if he was busy asking Jim to fly to Turkey with cash, somehow Nathan managed to fuck things up," Clint spoke up.

Aiden closed his eyes. What the hell were they thinking, taking Evie to Turkey with them? Dexter must have read his mind.

"Jim probably had no idea what his friend was into. He probably thought Nathan needed money for gambling debts."

"I don't care what he thought. Giving cash to somebody in a foreign country is too damned risky. This was a stupid decision on his part. If he wanted to do it, he shouldn't have taken Blake or Evie," Aiden bit out.

"No shit! So you confirmed he took money out of the bank in Turkey?" Drake asked.

"He did that six days ago," Clint answered.

"Evie stopped calling Trenda five days ago. So getting the cash didn't solve the problem."

"All three of them were checked into the same hotel. Blake checked them out four days ago. I haven't been able to find any record of them having checked in anyplace else."

"Foreign hotels always demand you check in with passports," Aiden said.

"Maybe they have blank South American passports that they're using," Drake said bitterly.

"Or maybe they're being held someplace," Dex put in. "We have a lock on where Nathan is. He's staying at a rundown hotel in Antakya. He checked in yesterday."

"Okay, then-" Drake started.

"I've got you both booked on a flight to Houston, then on to Istanbul. From there you're on a tin can to Hatay which is close to Antakya. That's where Jim withdrew the cash. You fly out of Tennessee in four hours to Houston," Lydia said.

Aiden looked around the friendly office. His eyes landed on a picture with Jim and Blake, with Evie in the middle. She looked so little. She should have been protected, and instead, Jim had put her in danger. His mind was going into hyperdrive wondering what was happening to her. Please God say it wasn't as bad as he thought it was.

* * *

Two hours later, he and Drake were at the McGhee Tyson airport waiting for their flight to Houston. Drake was on the phone with Trenda when Dexter called.

"Let me get Drake," Aiden stopped his friend. Aiden raised his hand, and Drake got off his phone call with his sister, knowing that Aiden was getting his attention for something important. They walked over to an empty spot next to one of the windows and put the phone on a low speaker volume. Dexter started talking.

"Got the phone records for Evie, Jim, and Blake's phones. I can see the texts. It's not good. Five days ago, there were two texts from Evie to both Blake and Jim's phones. It said: *HELP. SOMEONE IS AFTER ME WITH A GUN. WILL TRY TO GET TO EMBASSY.*"

Aiden put his hand on Drake's big shoulder and squeezed.

"Go on," Aiden prompted Dex.

"Multiple calls and texts went back to her phone from Jim and Blake's phone, and then finally there was a video from her phone to Jim's phone. It lasted for three and a half minutes. We don't have access to the video or the calls, just the times and duration. The texts were all in the same vein, they wanted to know where she was, and if she was safe."

"That was five days ago. What's transpired since then?" Aiden asked harshly. Two women looked up from where they were sitting in the waiting area. He needed to take it down a notch…or thirteen.

"There have been two more videos sent to Jim's phone, the last one thirty-six hours ago," Dexter said quietly. "It's not Evie sending the videos, this is being handled by someone sophisticated. Normally a video is uploaded with a link that we could then view. These three were sent directly to Jim's phone. Neither Clint nor I could hack it. It's as secure as a telephone call. We just show the record of it having been sent. This was sent by a professional."

The sharp taste of fear coated Aiden's tongue, as he considered all of the things that somebody might have filmed with Evie's phone and then sent to Jim.

"Why the fuck haven't these clowns answered our calls?" Drake yelled at the phone in Aiden's hand. "Obviously, they're taking calls! What the flying fuck?"

Out of the corner of his eye, Aiden could see a man getting up and looking at them. He then looked around the passenger area. The women at ticketing were staring at Drake as well.

"You need to keep it together, Buddy, otherwise they won't let you on the plane."

Drake closed his eyes and nodded. When he opened them, he was back to the in-control SEAL that Aiden knew he could be.

"Dex, since they're using their phones, have you been able to get a lock on their location?"

"They're powered down right now, but Clint and Lydia have it set to alert us immediately if they come back online. They'll have the best possible location identified once they turn on their phones," Dex assured Aiden.

"Why would they turn off their phones in the first place if they're getting communications from the kidnappers?" Drake asked. Then he sighed. "Scratch that. They're telling them the next time they'll contact them. They probably picked up burner phones in Turkey that they're using for day-to-day use."

"Most likely," Dex agreed.

"We'll let you know any and all updates when you land in Houston."

Chapter Seven

Lydia had managed to get them each window seats in the exit aisles, which meant they didn't sit together. Aiden didn't think they would have had much to say to one another anyway. The flight seemed to take forever, and he couldn't imagine how long the one to Turkey would feel like. They finally landed in Houston, and they headed toward baggage claim.

Aiden and Drake stopped short when they got off the escalator and saw a familiar face. It was Lieutenant Albert Riviera. He had a phone in his hand that he held out to Drake.

"Karen's fine," the man said. "Mason wants to talk to you."

Drake's face paled, but he stood tall as he listened to what Mason was telling him. Albert spoke to Aiden quietly.

"Karen was in a minor car accident and she's in surgery. There were complications with the pregnancy. I've got us on a plane to San Diego in an hour."

Aiden wasn't sure how Mason had arranged Albert's appearance, but he was thankful that the man was there.

Drake turned back to them. "I don't need a chaperone," he said quietly, as he handed the phone back to the lieutenant.

"Avery, I was on my way back to base. Mason knew I was here visiting my family, so he tagged me. You're stuck with me. We leave in an hour. I'll be back in just a minute." He walked toward the restrooms.

Drake and Aiden stared at one another.

"He told you?" Drake asked.

Aiden nodded.

"Karen was crying when they took her into surgery. She was begging them to save our little girl," the last words were choked out. "Mason said that even if the surgery works, it'll still be touch and go for a while. She's only five months along."

Aiden watched as Drake pulled it together. It was as if all of the man's will and concentration were with Karen.

"All of the women in your life are strong. They'll make it. You have to believe that." As soon as the words were out of his mouth, Aiden realized how badly he needed to believe it.

"Piper was in the car. Mason said she's barely holding it together. I need to call her, but before I do, I need to tell you something." Drake's fingers dug deeply into Aiden's shoulder. They would leave bruises.

"Shoot."

"You have one shot at this. You fucked up with my sister before. I don't know what went down between the two of you, but it was nothing compared to now. This is your shot at redemption. You fuck it up, don't bother coming back to the states. Are we clear?" Aiden looked into black eyes filled with fire, and he nodded.

There wasn't a chance in hell that he was going home without Evie by his side.

"You take care of your girls in San Diego. I'll bring Evie home. You have my word."

* * *

Aiden was used to going to sleep on a plane and waking up on the other side of the world, no matter how keyed up he was. He forced himself to do it this time as well. He'd need the sleep to be at full capacity when he landed.

Going through the airport in Istanbul toward his connecting flight, he was enveloped by a swarm of people. This was one of the world's largest airports, and the travelers seemed liked any others in the world, a combination of harried, weary, and agitated. But the airport personnel had a totally different attitude than what he was used to. They were suspicious, on guard, and, in some cases just out and out scared. Aiden wondered how many of them had lived through the terrorist attack that had killed and injured so many last year. He made an effort to smile, as he went up to the ticketing desk, despite everything swirling around in his own head.

"Your flight will depart in an hour, Mr. O'Malley," the woman said with a hint of an accent. "The lounge is down the hall and to your right." She pointed. "You can get your currency exchanged there."

There'd been four messages on his phone when he'd arrived, and now he wanted to return the calls. He didn't care if it was three a.m. in San Diego, Dexter and Gray would just have to deal with it.

He punched in Gray's number first and then swore when he got voice mail.

"Dammit, you better not be on a plane. If you're on a plane, when you land, you better head back to the United States. You're needed there." He disconnected then called Dexter.

"Yo."

"Why do you always sound awake no matter what time I call?" Aiden complained.

"Because I *am* awake," Dex said with a smile in his voice.

"What did Gray mean that he was on his way?"

"When he heard that your ass was flying solo, he hopped a plane," Dex answered.

"That's bullshit. With everything going on, he needs to be with the team."

"You and I both know, that if we are deployed, he'll already be close to where he needs to be anyway. So, shut the hell up, and let me tell you what I found out."

"Did they turn on their phones?"

Dexter didn't respond.

"Okay, I'm shutting up."

"I pulled up all of Nathan's phone records, and he's been calling a rare bookseller in Antakya. Not just his store, but the old guy's personal cell phone, and his store in Istanbul. When I say calling, I'm talking ten calls a day. Nathan is desperate for this guy."

"Still? I thought you said there wasn't any phone usage on Nathan's cell phone."

"It stopped three days ago. I figure he started using a burner phone. I did more digging. Somebody broke into the old guy's shop three days ago and tore it up. It was searched from top to bottom."

"How did you find this out?"

"I hacked the police report." How in the hell Dex managed to hack into the police department halfway around the world was beyond him.

"Is the owner okay?" Aiden asked.

"He hasn't been reached. Apparently, he's out of the country on a buying trip."

"I need the address of the shop."

"I already emailed you all of the details."

"Does this guy do buying trips to Iraq? Baghdad?" Aiden asked.

"Yep," Dex answered. "Are you thinking he might have smuggled the passports into Turkey?"

"That's what makes sense. I wonder if he knows that he's sitting on a goldmine."

"I doubt it. Nathan probably needed the thirty grand to pay him for some books that the passports were hidden in."

"That's my guess too," Aiden agreed. "That dumb asshole must have had the money to pay the bookdealer at some point and then lost it. That's when he needed to pull Jim into this mess."

"Seems to me that when he finally got the cash from Jim, the bookdealer was out of town, and that's when the buyer lost patience and snatched your girl for collateral."

Aiden kept thinking about the videos that the kidnappers had been sending to Jim's phone. He prayed that his imagination was worse than reality.

"Track down the bookdealer. I want to know exactly where he is by the time I touch down in Antakya, am I clear?"

"Already on it. It's a little more complicated because of the phone carriers in Turkey. Otherwise I would've already done it."

Aiden sighed. He knew Dex was doing the best he could.

"Keep your cell powered up and turned on, I want to track you at all times, are we clear?" Dex demanded.

"Yes, Mom. Did you boss our lieutenant around too?"

"He already knows the rules. You're the problem child."

"I'll keep it on," Aiden promised. He looked up at the monitor and saw his plane was getting ready to board. "Got to go. I will have to turn off the phone while I'm in the air. But other than that, I'll have it on."

"Good. Be safe. We'll get her home."

"From your lips to God's ears."

* * *

God, he hated small planes that weren't military, and this one was no exception. The pilot couldn't land worth a shit. But at least, it had taken his mind off Evie for five minutes.

Aiden checked into his hotel and dumped his gear. He checked, and there was a reservation for Gray Tyler as well. Figures.

As soon as he was done, he made his way to the hotel where Nathan was still checked in. His height and blond hair made him stick out like a sore thumb, but it didn't seem to matter to anyone. There was a total lack of interest at the seedy hotel.

Aiden didn't speak Turkish, and the man at the front desk didn't speak English, but finally, they found they could communicate in Arabic and money. He bartered, but eventually parsed out the equivalent of a hundred US dollars to be let into Nathan's hotel room. Three hours later, Nathan finally showed. He made enough noise coming down the hall, that Aiden easily got into place by the time he came into the room.

In one swift move, Aiden had the door slammed shut, Nathan on the floor, with his boot on the back of his neck, and Nathan's arms jammed up his back.

"Make a move, and I'll break your neck."

Nathan was stupid; he jerked up. Aiden pressed down hard with his boot until the man passed out. It was for the best, it gave him time to pat him down. Aiden found two knives and one Sig Sauer pistol that went along with the two clips of ammo that he'd found when he'd searched the room. He was an idiot, leaving that kind thing in a flea trap like this.

He used the dirty sheets from the bed to tie him to the one chair in the room, then he waited. During his search, he'd also found two phones. One was a smart phone, the other was a cheap burner. He called Dexter from the burner.

"Dex? This is Aiden."

"What's this number?" he asked.

"This is Nathan's burner phone. Can you track all the incoming and outgoing calls on it?"

"I'm on it. I'll call you on yours with all of the info. Give me twenty minutes."

"Just leave a message. I'm going to be busy."

"Got it. Give him hell." Dex hung up.

Nathan's breathing had changed while Aiden had been talking. He grabbed him by his ear and whispered. "I know you're awake. I need you to listen to me. You have one chance to avoid pain. I want to know everything, and I mean everything, you know about the operation that got Evie Avery kidnapped."

"I don't know what you're talking about," Nathan said, his eyes sly.

Aiden picked up the washrag he'd gotten from the bathroom earlier, and a ripped strip of sheet. He shoved it into Nathan's mouth and tied the strip around his head. Then he ripped open his shirt. He took the duller of the two knives, and pierced his flesh next to his right nipple and drew a line to his left nipple. Nathan's scream would have been heard throughout the hotel if he hadn't gagged him.

"Stop your whining."

The man was still yelling.

Aiden sat down on the corner of the bed, and watched as blood dripped down his chest. Nathan was trembling, but he finally stopped making noise behind his gag. Aiden stood back up.

"Don't make me open up your pants." Nathan's eyes went wide with terror, and tears spilled. "Are you ready to answer my questions?" Aiden asked in a calm voice.

Nathan nodded.

Aiden untied the gag.

"I don't know where she is. I swear to God, I don't know where she is."

"I believe you. But if you don't tell me everything you know, I won't kill you, I'll just make you wish you were dead."

"But I don't know anything, that's the problem," the man screeched.

"Calm down. Start from the beginning. Tell me why you're in Turkey. Tell me about your assignment."

"I don't know where the girl is. Jim's furious."

"Don't babble. Take a breath and tell me why you're here. What was your job?" Aiden waited for the man to get himself together.

"Meet with a man named Tanis, and make sure that the money was deposited into RLI's account. When we got half, then we show them the passports, and I was supposed to wait until the rest was deposited and hand over the passports."

"Okay, so what went wrong?"

His eyes shot sideways.

"Tell me."

"I should have already had the passports because I had fifty thousand USD to pay a bookseller for some rare books. He didn't know he was smuggling passports from Baghdad. But I'd lost half the money in a dice game."

Idiot!

"So that's when you contacted Jim?"

"He was my Hail Mary. I couldn't believe he was actually in Greece. God was smiling down on me. But when we had the money, we couldn't find the bookseller. He'd left the country. That was a week ago."

"How did Evie get involved?"

"She was never meant to. Tanis and his guys must have been following Jim and me when we went to the bank, and then followed him back to his hotel. When I didn't deliver the passports, they nabbed Evie."

"What have they threatened?"

His eyes slid sideways again. Aiden held up the knife.

"There were videos. They beat the hell out of her. We have two more days, and if we don't deliver the passports, they'll start cutting her up. They said she would only last two days after that started."

Aiden closed his eyes.

"Where are Jim and Blake?"

"They'll be back tonight. They went to Istanbul, the bookdealer has another store there."

"Are you still contacting the terrorists with the email address?" Aiden asked.

"How do you know that?" Nathan wanted to know.

"We know everything."

"Who are you?" Nathan finally thought to ask.

"I'm a friend of Evie's. Now, where is the cash to pay for the passports? You only had a few Turkish Lira on you."

"Jim has it. He didn't trust me with it."

"At last, he shows some sense."

"I'm sorry about the girl. I really am. You have to know, I want this deal to go through as much as you do. I don't want her hurt, I swear I don't. But if this goes sideways, these guys will come after me next. And if they don't get me, then my friends in Africa will kill me for fucking it up. I'll do anything to make this right."

Aiden looked at the loser in front of him and realized he was telling the truth.

"I'm a good man to have in a fight," he wheedled.

"You're a screw-up."

"But you need as many people working on this as possible."

What he needed was this guy to stay out of his way, and not cause any problems while Aiden made his play.

Aiden put down the dull knife and picked up the sharp one, and watched as the guy's eyes widened. "I don't think you really understand where the true danger lies. If you want to stay alive, you stay out of this. You let me handle it. You get the hell out of Turkey today. If I ever see you again after you leave this room, you're a dead man."

Nathan swallowed. "But-"

Aiden clapped his hand over Nathan's mouth and then made a quick cut across his nipple.

"If you do anything to trip me up, I will cut you, just like they plan to cut Evie. And I will enjoy it. Are we clear?"

Aiden didn't need to wait for his answer, it was written all over Nathan's face. He took his palm off of Nathan's mouth, and turned for the door.

"Aren't you going to untie me?"

"No. You're an Army Ranger, you'll figure it out."

Chapter Eight

When he got out to the street, he flagged down a taxi. He got in and listened to his message from Dex. There were texts going back and forth from the burner phones, and it confirmed that Jim and Blake were due back tonight. It also said where they were staying. Dex also said that Gray had already landed in Antakya. After everything he had learned, he'd be lying if he didn't admit he was happy that his friend would be there to help.

He called Dexter.

"When was the last video sent?" he asked without preamble.

"Yesterday local time to you," Dex answered.

"How many hours ago. I want a countdown. We have forty-eight hours from the time it was sent."

Dex didn't ask for what. "That leaves us with thirty hours." Aiden checked his watch. It was Tuesday at six pm. He had until Wednesday at midnight, if they stuck to their schedule, which he couldn't trust.

"I'll have Gray filled in by the time you hit the hotel. Hopefully, he'll be there by the time you arrive. His ETA is about the same as yours."

"Why am I not surprised?"

"I'm still trying to hack into the local carrier so that I can track down the bookseller." Dexter hung up. Despite the breakneck speed of the taxi, Aiden still wished he would speed up. It seemed like the second hand was spinning around on his watch dial.

They came to an abrupt halt two blocks from the hotel when there was a traffic jam.

"Let me out here, I'll walk the rest of the way."

The driver looked at him in confusion. Aiden repeated himself in Arabic. He still didn't understand. Finally, Aiden just threw some bills at him and got out of the cab. He jogged to the hotel. Gray was waiting in the lobby.

"Tell me. Why the timeline?" were the first words out of his Lieutenants mouth.

The two tall, fair Americans were garnering attention. "Let's go to my room," Aiden said. They headed toward the elevator. Once inside, Gray looked Aiden over. He knew that he was not as composed as he normally was.

As soon as the hotel room door closed, Gray turned on him. "Spit it out."

"They're going to start cutting on her in thirty hours." Aiden looked at his watch. "Twenty-nine and a half hours now. We have to meet with them, but I don't know if they'll have her with them, and if we go in without the passports, I think they'll just call whoever has her, and she's dead. But she could end up dead even if we deliver. Our only call is to rescue her."

"Agreed. What has Dexter found?"

"We need to get them to send another message from Evie's cell phone and then pinpoint that location, but that just means she's going to be hurt some more." For once Aiden's anguish bled through.

"Better now than at the deadline," Gray consoled. Aiden wanted to hit him. "Another request for proof of life?" Gray asked, reading Aiden's mind.

"Yeah." Aiden turned to the bed and emptied his jacket pockets. "I only have a pistol and two knives."

"I have a former Air Force buddy who was stationed at Incirlik meeting me at the Antakya bazaar in an hour. We'll be covered."

"Shit, he's really taking a risk."

"He knows what's at stake. Do we wait for those friends of Evie's? What are their names?"

"Blake and Jim. They will be here after we get the firepower. My gut says yes. They're just as invested in getting her back. I'll deal with them after she's safe."

Gray nodded.

"I brought something to darken our hair."

Aiden was used to that, he just hadn't had time to pick up the supplies when he'd left the states. Gray with his light hair that was going silver needed the hair color as much as he did.

They applied the color, then Gray left to meet his buddy. Meanwhile, Aiden checked in with Dexter. This time he got a conference call with Dex, Clint, and Lydia.

"How's Karen?" he asked.

"She's doing fine, so is the baby. They're keeping her overnight. I think Drake is doing worse than she is. I highly doubt she'll be allowed to walk for the duration of her pregnancy if Drake has anything to say about it." Lydia laughed.

Aiden shook his head. Only a woman would be able to laugh at something that had been so dire just hours ago.

"Seriously, though," Clint jumped in. "They say with the right care their little girl will go full term."

"That's really good news," Aiden said sincerely.

"What's going on with Evie?" Lydia asked.

Aiden balked at the idea of telling a non-military person, and a woman, what was going on. Lydia must have sensed it.

"Aiden, I'm a big girl, who has been held and tortured by drug dealers. I'm already imagining the worst. Tell me."

"We have less than twenty-eight hours before they say they'll begin cutting her to prove they're serious. We have to pinpoint her location and go in. I don't believe that they'll release her even if we find and turn over the passports."

"Good, don't trust the motherfuckers," Lydia said vehemently. "How will you find her?"

"You're my ace in the hole. I need to get them to turn on Evie's phone again, and you need to trace it fast. Then Gray, Blake, Jim, and I are going to go in and take her back."

"How are you going to get them to turn on the phone?" Clint asked.

"We've got to convince them to send another video before they get to the torture part."

"Do you have an idea?" Dexter asked.

"Yeah. Can any of you plant a story that there was a Caucasian woman found dead? That will allow us to demand proof of life."

Aiden listened as the three of them discussed ideas on how to upload stories onto the internet. It got gruesome as Clint searched for pictures that they could use. Lydia found a friend that was able to get the story translated into Turkish.

"Give us two hours, and it will be all over Turkey," Clint promised.

"Perfect."

"Then I'll send an email from Nathan's phone demanding proof of life." Aiden prayed they wouldn't hurt Evie in the process.

"Expect a call from Drake," Lydia warned.

Aiden called Jim on his burner phone.

"Where are you?"

"Who is this?"

"This is Aiden O'Malley. I'm in Antakya, at the Anemon Hotel. How far away are you?" He heard some muffled talking, then Blake was on the line.

"We'll be there in an hour and a half."

"Make it an hour." Aiden hung up.

He looked down at his watch. At his calculations, the men should show up about the same time Gray returned to the room, which would dovetail with the techie's story plant.

He picked up his own cell phone that had vibrated when he had called Jim. He saw Drake's name and called him back.

"Why the fuck didn't you answer?" Drake immediately demanded.

"I was talking to Jim."

"You mean he finally deigned to pick up his phone? How fucking nice of him. You're going to kill the motherfucker, aren't you?"

Aiden tamped down the fury he'd been feeling as he'd talked to Jim Sellers. There was no point in letting Drake reignite it, he needed to stay focus and use all available resources to rescue Evie.

"I'm going to take care of that problem after we rescue your sister."

"Clint told me about your plan. It sounds slicker than snot," Drake praised.

Please, Jesus, let it work.

"I hope so. How is Karen? The baby?"

"They're fine. You call me the second you have Evie. The second! You don't fuck this up."

"I won't."

The line went dead.

Aiden grinned wryly.

Now was one of the hardest parts of any mission…the waiting.

Aiden sat down in the chair next to the window and peered out, but he found himself reliving his time with Evie. God, she was amazing. Breathtaking. A pain in the ass. He smiled as got lost in his thoughts.

* * *

Flashback, Tennessee, Three Months Ago

The room smelled fresh and clean from the fabric softener, but Evie's alluring scent permeated the air as well.

"Need help?" Aiden asked.

"Are you offering to fold clothes?" she asked. Her surprise was obvious.

He picked up the top sheet and handed her a corner. He grinned at her. "Trenda told me that you were down here."

"I'm more than capable of doing the laundry by myself."

"Never thought you couldn't, Kitten."

"Then why are you here?" She snagged his corner and continued to fold the pale green sheet.

"Just here to help and keep you company. Maybe get a couple of answers."

"Shouldn't you be monitoring the alarm system or something?"

He fished a remote out of his pocket. "I've got everything I need right here. Now, why are you so prickly about letting somebody help you?"

"It's not the help, it's the questions."

He bent and picked up the basket of clean clothes and put it on the dryer. "Here, I'll fold these clothes, that should make the questions painless."

"Stop! Those are the unmentionables."

Aiden laughed and watched Evie blush. "Hell, I don't think I've ever heard someone say unmentionables outside of a movie. That's adorable."

She shoved the rest of the sheets at him. "Here, fold these. I'll fold the underwear. Now, what are your questions?"

He paused.

"Just spit it out already. I'm not going to bite," she growled at him.

"Kitten, I wouldn't object if you did," he said with a slow grin.

Evie's blush deepened, and Aiden grinned wider. He loved how her porcelain skin gave her away.

"I don't know any more about why Dad's after Piper than what we discussed at dinner last night."

"I'm not asking about that."

"You want to know about Drake? Hell, big brother has been out of my life for years. Since you and he work on the SEAL teams together, you know more about him than I do."

"Don't want to know anything more about your brother."

He watched as she shuffled her lavender bikini panties to the bottom of the basket. He raised his eyebrow, to show that he had caught her.

"Dammit, you weren't supposed to see that," she huffed.

"Is lavender your favorite color? I would think so, since it's your middle name."

"Go fuck yourself."

"Language. You don't want to end up owing Bella more money," Aiden admonished.

"Just tell me what you want to know."

She was so tiny, so beautiful, so fierce. "How long have you been the family guardian?"

Evie hesitated mid-fold. Then she let her dark curls fall over her face. "I don't know what you're talking about," she mumbled.

He tucked her hair behind her ear, then lifted her chin so that they were looking at one another.

"I want to know how long you've been looking out for every one of your sisters."

"Seriously. I don't," she protested.

"I call bullshit. Piper told me how you're just like Drake, funneling money to everyone. That's why you live at the hotel and are basically working sixty hours a week, and taking on as many side jobs as possible. She also explained that when Maddie's boyfriend wouldn't leave her alone, you went up to school and had words with him, and suddenly he stopped bothering her."

"Piper sure does talk a lot."

"So, tell me how long you've been the family protector."

"Seriously, I just help out occasionally. Mostly I mind my own business."

"I've known you for three days, and I know that to be the biggest lie I've heard in two years. You never stay out of anybody's business. You are what my grandmother O'Malley would have called a buttinsky."

"Well, thank you for nothing!" Evie wrenched her chin away from his grip.

Aiden's arms came around her in a soft hug.

"I meant that as a compliment."

"Sure didn't sound like one."

He considered her, part of him wanted to pick her up and put her on the dryer so that they would be eye to eye, but he didn't want to use his strength when sparring with her. No, he would continue to pit his will against hers.

He dipped his forehead against hers and their breath mingled. "It was a compliment, Kitten. Your loyalty is a turn on. It's scary as hell. How did you get Maddie's boyfriend to back off?"

Her eyes skidded away from his.

"Eyes, Baby."

She looked back at him. "A bat," she said softly.

It took him a moment to process what she'd said.

"Dammit, you used a bat to threaten the bastard?"

"I didn't threaten him. I hit him with it. I broke his wrist."

"Dammit, Eva, that's assault, you could have ended up in jail."

"Maddie had a black eye! I told him next time I would break both his knees. The motherfucker believed me."

"Jesus. You're not even five feet tall."

"I'm five foot one!"

"You could have been hurt. Hell, he'd already hit Maddie."

"I took him by surprise, and I had a bat. I also took pepper spray with me. I was covered."

Aiden shuddered. The woman had no fear. He still remembered how she came at him with nothing but a mop.

"Don't ever do something like that again."

"Who died and made you the boss of me?" Evie demanded as she struggled to get out of his arms.

All of Aiden's good intentions went out the window. He held her in place and slanted his mouth over hers.

Fire ignited.

Evie gripped the front of his shirt, and he clasped the back of her delicate neck, massaging her straining muscles as she arched closer. Her lips parted. Their kiss turned wet and wild.

Aiden felt pinpricks in his scalp at the same time Evie nipped at his tongue. His eyes slammed open, and he saw her flushed face. In no way was she fighting, no, his hellcat was as turned on as he was. He picked her up, and she wrapped her legs around his waist. No woman had ever caught fire like Eva Avery.

His ears started to ring.

He gripped her ass and pulled her closer. He was in a vortex of need, and the bells wouldn't stop.

"Aiden," Evie said as she pushed against his shoulders.

He looked down at her beautiful face. It was then he realized that the buzzer on the dryer was ringing. He choked out a laugh. She grinned up at him.

"I don't have words, Eva."

"I do. Let me down. I have laundry to finish." She sounded so prim and proper with her honeyed Southern accent, but her hair was messed, her eyes were glittering, and her lips were swollen.

"I'll help."

"You're banned from the laundry room. I think Trenda needs help getting supper started."

Aiden laughed. "That's not going to be nearly as fun," he said as he left the small room.

Chapter Nine

Aiden stood up with a gun in his hand when there was a knock on the door. He checked the peephole and saw Gray. He had a backpack that he hadn't had before.

"What's new?" Gray asked as he got into the room.

"Dex and the team have a plan in place where we should be good to demand proof of life in an hour or two."

"Will it be solid?" Gray questioned.

Aiden explained it. Gray winced when Aiden described the picture of the corpse that Clint had found.

"Okay, that will work. Anything else?"

"Jim and Blake should arrive any minute."

Gray gave Aiden a level stare. "Are you still good with having them in on this operation?"

"I checked them out months ago when I was in Tennessee. Their reputations are strong."

"But?"

"As soon as this is over, game over," Aiden said softly.

Gray nodded. He shrugged the backpack off his shoulders and dropped it onto the carpeted floor with a clunk. "Let's divvy up the toys."

They were going over the weapons when there was a call on Nathan's phone.

"Yeah?" Aiden answered.

"We're here. What room are you in?"

"Five-oh-seven."

Gray and Aiden tucked away what they needed, then left out two pistols on the bed for Blake and Jim.

"You haven't met them before, have you?" Gray said.

"Nope, but I've seen pictures. I'll recognize them."

Gray nodded.

Aiden's phone rang when the knock sounded on the door. It was Dexter. He handed the phone to Gray and checked the peephole. He easily recognized the two men. They looked ragged.

He threw open the door.

"Why the fuck didn't you answer your phones? Why didn't you call Drake?" So much for calm and cool. Aiden sucked in a deep breath.

"I thought we could handle this," Jim said.

"We fucked up," Blake said at the same time.

Aiden looked over his shoulder at Gray. "Things are in place, do you want me to put it on speaker?" he asked.

Aiden focused on the phone and nodded.

"Dex, we have Jim Sellers and Blake Tenkin here. Take it from the top," Gray requested.

"The plan is to demand another proof of life," Dex said from the phone.

"They'll never go for it," Jim broke in as he sank down onto the bed. His grief was palpable. "They'll just start hurting her sooner. Don't do it." He looked up at Aiden pleadingly.

"Stop it," Blake bit out. "Aiden wouldn't be here if he didn't care. He won't have some half-assed plan. Let him explain."

"Keep quiet," Gray glared at Blake and Jim. Both men stilled at Gray's command. "Dex, continue."

"It's all over every Turkish news site that a Caucasian woman was found in the Antakya landfill. She matches the description of Evie."

"How in the hell did you manage that?" Jim asked.

"I told you to keep your mouth shut. Don't make me say it again," Gray commanded.

Jim nodded.

"When you ask for proof of life. Ask for more than a video. Demand to talk to her, say that a video could have been previously recorded. Keep her talking," Dex directed them. "She has a smart phone, so we should only need thirty seconds, but the longer we have to pinpoint the signal, the better."

"Can we take a call now?" Aiden asked.

"Yeah, we're ready on our end."

"Jim, they call your phone, right?"

Jim nodded and pulled his phone out of his jean's pocket.

"Don't be a shit. Talk to them," Blake said.

"Yeah, they call me on this phone."

"Do you have the videos on it?" Aiden asked.

"Don't look," Dex said.

"He's right. Don't look," Blake concurred. "Evie's going to make it. She's tough. Now that we have a plan, we're going to get her."

Aiden looked at Jim, his jaw was trembling.

"Jim, are they used to talking to you?"

The man nodded.

"Okay. Expect a call. Dex, send the email."

"But we don't have the passports," Jim protested.

"Think it through, Jim," Blake said. He was clearly upset with his partner. "Right now we aren't contacting them with delivery, we just want proof of life."

"Oh yeah. That's right."

Jesus. The man was a basket case, Aiden thought with disgust.

"The email is sent. I copied links to the articles. I'll call you when they pick it up."

* * *

It was the longest three hours of Aiden's life. Gray arranged for food to be sent up to the room since Jim and Blake hadn't eaten since they'd left Istanbul. Everybody needed to be fueled up for the mission.

Jim didn't talk at all. Blake explained that they had paid the landlord of Tahaf Books to let them in for a price. They had spent the last day and a half going through the entire store looking for the passports. Finally, they had gotten ahold of the bookdealer, Mehmet Tahaf, on his mobile phone. He said he would be back in Antakya in three days. He had Nathan's special order with him.

It was three and a half hours before Dex called. Aiden lunged for the phone on the dresser.

"They picked up the email. I asked for a FaceTime call. They said they would arrange it in ten minutes. Remember, keep her talking," Dex reminded Aiden.

"Got it."

Aiden had already watched the three videos. The first had been fine. The second two had made him want to howl. He'd kept it together…just. He was still trying to wrap his head around the fact that she had mentioned him. There she was, facing death, and she mentioned him. God, what had he thrown away?

He had to focus on the mission. He would get her out of there. Then he would exact retribution on everyone involved. His eyes shot over to Jim, who jerked under the weight of his stare.

The distinctive ring of a FaceTime call sounded.

Jim answered. "Hello, let me talk to Evie."

"You have one minute," a man answered. He had an English accent. Aiden had already memorized it.

Evie came on screen. Her face was a mass of bruises. "Jim?" she whispered through a swollen jaw.

"Honey," he choked out. "Oh, Sweetheart," he didn't seem to know what to say. Blake took the phone from him.

"Evie. It's going to be all right. We're getting the passports. Everything is going to be just fine," he said firmly.

"Really?" The word came out garbled.

"Yes. You need to hang on."

"When?"

"Tomorrow morning," he lied.

Aiden watched from off screen as her face crumpled. "Thank you."

"Enough." The phone was taken from her. Once again all they saw was the wall of her room she was being held in. "What time tomorrow can we expect receipt?" the man asked.

"Ten a.m."

"We will call you with delivery instructions at nine a.m. Have your phone turned on." The man disconnected the call.

Jim was trying not to cry. Blake put his arm around his shoulders. "She's going to be fine. We'll get her."

Dex was still on the line with Gray, and he had been listening in. "We have their location. They're fourteen miles from you." He rattled off an address. "I'll have more information on the neighborhood and building before you get there."

"Thanks," Gray said, before disconnecting the call and following Aiden out the door of the hotel room. Blake led the way since it had been decided he would drive.

They all folded into the gray Fiat. It was a little after midnight, so the traffic was light. Gray had the address loaded into his phone, and he was in the front seat providing directions to Blake. They drove by the building, parked two blocks away in a narrow alley, and then called Dexter.

"Can't read the signs on the building. But it looks like an auto body shop to me," Gray said.

"You got it in one," Dex confirmed. "It went out of business last year."

Aiden didn't know how Dexter had gotten the information, but he trusted him.

"I don't have the blueprints."

"We can take it from here," Gray assured him.

"Call when you've secured her. I'll direct you to the correct hospital. There is an American doctor expecting her. I'll also wake up somebody at the Embassy."

"Gotta go," Aiden said from the backseat as he opened his car door. He was in charge of the mission. They could talk about her aftercare as soon as she was safe.

The three other men got out of the car just as quietly as he did, and melted into the night, with Aiden in the lead. When they got to the back of the auto body shop, there was a chain link fence around the lot that contained at least ten cars in various states of repair. There were three garage doors leading to car bays, as well as an office door.

"Looks like they're still in business," Jim said softly.

"Look closer," Gray pointed. Every car had dirt and rust on them. "They haven't been touched in forever."

Jim nodded.

Aiden softly rattled the fence.

"What the fuck are you doing?" Jim hissed.

"He's checking for a dog," Gray whispered in exasperation.

When moments passed, and there was no barking Aiden figured it was safe. "Okay, Gray, you're with Blake, go left. Jim and I will go right, we'll meet in front. Let's determine where we want to enter."

As they followed the fence around to the right, Jim pointed out the ladder that led to the roof, it was next to a padlocked side entrance. There were no windows on that side of the building. Aiden motioned for Jim to climb the ladder and check out the roof. He waited.

When Jim returned, he was grinning.

"There is a skylight into the garage. I could break it and drop in, it's not too far of a drop. We just need to have the timing tight."

Aiden nodded.

They paused at the corner of the building. Gray was at the front of the building. He was inspecting the front entrance, then came over to them. "Blake is headed back toward the rear. Let's go." They jogged to where Blake was waiting outside the fence.

"There were no points of entry on the left side of the building, no windows, no nothing," Blake reported.

"The front entrance is boarded shut," Gray explained.

Jim explained about the skylight.

"I'll be right back," Aiden was over the fence before the others could blink. He made his way carefully to the building using the cars as cover. Finally, he ran the last ten yards to the office. He peeked into the office window and saw two men at the desk playing dominoes. The middle garage door wasn't totally closed, so he slid over and peered under. There were three doors along the left wall, behind where the office was. He assumed at least one of them was a bathroom. No other doors. That had to be where Evie was being held. He waited and listened. He heard the faint sounds of Turkish being spoken. No English.

One of the three doors opened and a man came out, zipping his pants. Bile rose up his throat, but Aiden forced it down. He needed to be ice cold to help Evie. She didn't need his emotions.

The man went into the office with the two domino players. It was time to move. He made his way back to the chain link fence in less than a minute.

"Gray and Jim, go through the skylight." He looked at his watch. "We'll do this in exactly four minutes. Blake, you're with me. There are three men in the office. Behind the office are three doors, I'm almost a hundred percent sure that Evie is being held in one of those rooms."

All three men nodded. Blake quietly jumped the fence. Gray and Jim glided to the right. Aiden and Blake waited behind a rusted-out Buick for three minutes and thirty seconds. At the four-minute mark, Aiden kicked in the door, and he heard a crash. The two men who had been playing dominoes scrambled for the guns on the desk, and Blake and Aiden fired kill shots. The third man had a gun in his hand. Aiden shot him in the forehead.

"Clear!" Gray shouted from the garage.

"Found her!" Jim shouted.

Gray was holding open a door, it wasn't the one that the man had come out of. Before Aiden could go in, Gray grabbed his arm. "Brace," Gray warned.

"Let me go," Aiden growled.

He was assaulted by hideous stink.

"Evie, it's me, Jim."

"Get away," Evie said in a garbled Southern accent. "Please not again."

Aiden looked for a light switch. He eventually found one. A spare bulb shone a weak light in the dank room. Jim sat cross-legged on the floor with Evie on his lap. She struggled in his hold. Aiden crouched beside the duo.

"Evie, it's me, Aiden."

"Aiden?" she said softly. "Aiden?"

"Yeah, Kitten, it's me." He gently brushed his fingertips across her bruised cheek.

One of her eyes was swollen shut, but one brown eye clearly assessed him.

"You look good as a brunette," she lisped. "More intelligent."

He allowed himself to smile at her humor, knowing that she wanted him to, but she was killing him. They needed to get her to a hospital.

"Hand her to me." He scooped her out of Jim's arms.

"I can walk," she protested half-heartedly, but then she ruined it by groaning in pain.

"Hush. Where does it hurt?"

"I'm fine." He had trouble understanding her.

"Oh, Baby," he actually thought he might cry. He'd seen the beating. Why had he even bothered to ask where it hurt, it had to hurt everywhere.

She could only lift one arm part way to hold onto his shirt. He moved past Gray and raised his eyebrow.

"Blake's already taken the boards off the front entrance. He's bringing the car around to the front. I've notified Dex to have the doc ready, and he's calling the Embassy."

Evie's small body curled into him. "Can't I just go home?" she whispered softly.

"Eva, you need to get to a hospital, and you know it."

"Handsome, I need to get out of this country. Please take me home." He could hear tears in her voice.

Jim was hovering at his elbow. "Evie, you need to go to the hospital. Honey, you're hurting. You might have internal injuries."

She whimpered.

Aiden glared at the man.

"It's going to be all right. You're a hellcat, remember? We'll get you back to the states as quick as possible."

"Where's Drake?" She squirmed around in his arms.

"Karen?" she asked worriedly.

"He's home with Karen. She and the baby are fine, but she was in a small car accident. He needed to be with her."

Evie settled back down. It was as if she lost all of her strength. Her head dropped against his chest. Her breath rattled and then she passed out.

"We need to get her to the hospital. Now."

Chapter Ten

Evie was in and out of consciousness the entire ride to the hospital. She didn't look anything like his mother, but he couldn't help but see the similarities between the two women who had been so badly hurt.

But Evie was alive. He had to focus on that.

Doctor Invins was waiting outside the Emergency entrance with an orderly and a gurney.

"What can you tell me?" he asked Aiden.

"She just passed out about ten minutes ago. She's been able to talk. She's favoring her right side. I think she has broken ribs."

"Okay, we've got it from here. There's a woman from the Embassy waiting for you inside."

Aiden followed the gurney through the sliding doors. It wasn't until they took her through the back doors and Dr. Invins waved him off that he stopped. "I'll come out as soon as I have news," the doctor assured Aiden.

They had decided in the car that Gray would do all of the talking. They would not be explaining where and how they rescued Evie. Let the Turkish police deal with the human trash at the auto dealership. The doctor had been prepped and knew that Evie needed to be ambulatory as quickly as possible.

Gray was responsible for getting Evie cleared to leave the country. They needed to get her a temporary passport since hers was missing.

Aiden finally spared a glance at Blake and Jim. They were arguing in the corner of the waiting room. Blake was pissed.

He walked over to them. If he made a scene, if he did anything that called attention to them, he would put himself in jeopardy and not be able to help Evie. He had to keep his head. But once they were back in the states all bets were off. He would end them.

Jim was clutching Blake's arm, he shook it off and strode over to Aiden.

"Don't hurt Jim."

Aiden looked past Blake to the former Marine who was bigger than he was. He looked depleted.

"Don't do this, Tenkin. Don't stand in the way of what needs to happen."

"I love him," Blake's blue eyes pleaded with him.

"Doesn't matter. He's done. Don't be collateral damage. Leave the country now."

"We can't. We have to wait for Evie."

"She's got people who care. People who would never put her at risk. You need to leave."

All the color left Blake's face.

"I'll deal with Jim when I get back to the States."

"I'll stand with him. I knew better."

Aiden paused. "Yes. Yes, you did," Aiden agreed.

Blake turned toward Jim, then back to Aiden. "Remember on the first video. We saw the Englishman. He wasn't there tonight."

"I know. Now get the hell out of here. I can't stand the sight of him." Aiden turned to look at Gray.

* * *

Gray had called Drake from the car. Now Aiden called him.

"What did the doctor say?" Drake sounded frantic.

"She's going to be okay. She was giving me shit. She told me that I lacked intelligence. Your sister is one of the original hard-headed Avery women."

"Don't bullshit me, O'Malley. What was done to her?" Aiden heard the tentative tone and knew the real question Drake was asking.

"She had her clothes on. But they're doing a full exam. Drake, she sustained multiple beatings. I think she has broken ribs."

He heard Drake's gasp of pain. Then he heard a feminine whisper in the background, he was sure it was Karen.

"Get her home. Bring her to me."

"She'll want to go to Tennessee," Aiden protested.

"I want her in California. Karen can't travel. Did you make those bastards pay?"

"Three of them are dead."

"Jim and Blake. Are you going to kill them?"

"I'll take care of them once we're stateside."

"Let me."

"No. You stay with Karen and your baby. They're mine."

"Think what you want, O'Malley, but she's my sister."

Aiden pinched the bridge of his nose. He heard more whispers.

"When will you know her condition?"

That was the question of the hour. "I don't know."

"Clint said that a good doctor is working on her."

"Seems to be, if he'd ever get the hell back out here and tell us what's going on." Out of the corner of his eye, he saw Gray giving him a nod of encouragement. It didn't help. Nothing would help until he heard that Evie was going to be okay.

"Call me as soon as you hear something. I mean immediately. You got that?" Aiden didn't bristle at Drake's attitude, he knew how upset the man was.

"I will."

"I want her brought to California. She can double up with Piper," Drake said decisively.

That was so not happening. She'd be staying with him, Aiden thought.

"I'll call you."

"Don't forget." For once Drake sounded less like a commanding asshole and more like a distraught big brother.

"I won't," Aiden assured him.

He hung up and turned to Gray. "Goddammit, what's taking so long?"

Gray put his hand on Aiden's shoulder and squeezed. "I've done some checking. This place is good. Invins is good."

"Blake was right, she could have internal injuries. I swear she had broken ribs. If she does, they won't release her to fly commercial."

"I thought they only did that if the lungs collapsed," Gray said.

"They'll be cautious."

"We transport injured to Germany all the time with broken ribs. We'll arrange for her to fly out of Incirlik Air Force base, through Germany, to San Diego. We *will* get her stateside. Count on it."

"What did the woman from the Embassy say?" Aiden asked.

"The copy of Evie's passport that you brought helped. Amy will have a replacement for Evie in forty-eight hours."

Aiden nodded.

Two more hours passed.

Invins came out with a woman in scrubs. Shit, they'd operated. Aiden was beside them in a heartbeat.

"Tell me."

"We removed her spleen. She's doing well," the woman answered with accented English. "Her left kidney was bruised, but it will heal."

Okay. Okay, this was workable.

"What else?" He looked back and forth between the two doctors.

"The rape kit came back negative. She has a concussion, her shoulder was dislocated and we taped it up. Her ribs are badly bruised. No broken bones."

"We're taking her home in two days."

"Impossible," the female doctor said immediately.

Dr. Invins jumped in. "This is a special set of circumstances, Doctor. It is imperative that Ms. Avery be relocated back home as soon as possible."

"I won't release her."

"She's going home," Aiden said quietly.

Gray stepped up beside him. She looked at the two of them.

"Three days," she said.

"Two. She'll be going on military transport. She'll have the best care available."

The doctor sighed. "Fine."

"When can I see her."

"She'll be out of recovery and in a room in forty-five minutes."

Aiden nodded.

* * *

Aiden forgot just how tiny she was. She had such a big presence. Half of her face was bruised, but the rest was as white as the sheet she was lying on.

"Kitten?"

The eye that wasn't swollen shut fluttered open.

"Hi, handsome," she whispered, and then started coughing. He picked up the glass of water beside her bedside and put the straw to her lips. When she tried to raise her head, he put his arm under her pillow and lifted her.

"Take a slow sip."

He watched as her throat moved. After four swallows, he took the glass away.

"I want more," she protested.

"In a couple of minutes." Then because he couldn't help himself, he brushed a butterfly kiss against her bruised temple.

"Don't do that."

"Why not?"

"If you're tender, I'll feel fragile, and I'll cry. Don't let me cry."

"Oh, Baby, you have every right to cry."

"If I start, I might never stop." A tear seeped out of her swollen eye. "Oh, God, it's starting."

"I won't tell anybody."

"You're somebody." Her lower lip trembled. He looked at the cut that bisected the flesh. Ice pervaded his veins. One more man needed to die. He needed to find the man with the English accent, the man who commanded that she be beaten.

"Aiden?"

"I'm here." He knelt beside the bed, and continued to keep his arm under her pillow. He cupped her unblemished cheek. "I'm always going to be here, Eva."

"No, you won't. You left." More tears fell.

"I came back."

"Sure you did, you're a hero. You came to rescue the damsel in distress. Of course, you came back," she said bitterly. She turned her head away.

"Eyes."

She didn't respond.

"Please, Kitten."

She turned her head.

"Eye. I only have one good eye to look at you with."

He felt a glimmer of a grin. "Okay, I want to see your expression on me. I need it, Eva."

"What do you want?"

"I want you to listen to me. Really *hear* me."

She stared at him.

"Nothing would stop me from coming to you. I'm always going to be there when you need me."

She continued to stare at him.

"You're coming home with me."

She jerked her head, shaking it. "No way."

"Drake wants you in California."

"I'm going home to Tennessee. Trenda is going to take care of me."

"Drake wants you to stay with him. He intends for you to share a room with Piper."

"I'm going home to Tennessee," she said mutinously. Then she coughed again.

Aiden reached over and picked up the glass. "Drink."

"I want more this time." She pouted.

"God, you're stubborn."

She sipped from the straw. He waited until she finished this time.

"If I'm that much of a pain in the ass, then you should let me go to Tennessee."

Aiden laughed. "I thought you were a pain in the ass last night."

She searched his face. "Really?" she asked softly. He'd hurt her feelings.

"Yep, I also thought you were amazing and breathtaking."

"No, you didn't."

He put down the glass, and pulled her closer, treating her like spun glass.

"Eva, whether you're on the floor playing with Bella, watching a chick flick with Piper, going after some bastard with a bat, or you're catching fire in my arms, you have always taken my breath away."

She looked up at him with a dazed expression. "Handsome, I want to believe you. But you betrayed me."

"Wrong, I tried to protect you."

"Explain it to me." She yawned.

He brushed a light kiss across her lips. "Sleep, Kitten."

"Will you be here when I wake up?"

"I promise."

He watched as her she drifted to sleep.

* * *

The crew at Incirlik Air Force base was good, even though they weren't Navy. Invins had arranged for an ambulance to transport Evie all the way to the base, which was a feat in and of itself. The Turkish government wanted to sweep her kidnapping under the rug and avoid publicity. They were still dealing with an unsubstantiated story that had made international news about a European woman who supposedly had been found in the Antakya landfill, and they didn't want any more bad press.

As Gray and Aiden followed the ambulance in a small rental car, there were very few words spoken. Gray had found a radio station that played European techno music that Aiden had promptly shut off.

"You're no fun."

"And your point is?" Aiden asked.

"She's going to be fine," Gray assured him.

"There are lots of complications that can happen with a splenectomy. What's more, the doctor was right, she probably shouldn't be travelling so soon."

"She definitely shouldn't be flying commercial. This is military medical transport. This is what they do. She'll be fine. She'll be better than fine. She'll be in San Diego in no time, and surrounded by family."

Aiden looked at his phone. Ninety more minutes and they'd be at the base, and he'd be able to check on Evie. He knew that they'd given her a sedative for the drive. It was supposed to last three more hours, but she was stubborn. There was an attendant riding in the back with her. He would administer more if she woke up. Aiden prayed she wasn't in anymore pain.

"We'll get there soon," Gray said as he turned the radio back on. This time it was a Pink Floyd song. Aiden closed his eyes and calmed down. Gray was right, they'd be in San Diego in less than twenty hours.

* * *

The medics on the transport were thoroughly sick of him by the time they arrived in San Diego. He didn't know how often he heard the words, 'Stand down' and 'We've got this.' Finally, their captain just let him take point on Evie's care. When they unloaded her and got to the base hospital in Coronado, she was once again regaining consciousness.

"Where am I?" she asked in a panicked voice as she was wheeled into her room.

"You're home, Baby. You're in California," Aiden reassured her.

"Senior Chief, I need you to leave while I examine my patient," a doctor said as he came into the room.

Aiden stood straight. "I think you and I need to talk first. I'm a medic. She's been under my care while she was transported here. I have her records from Turkey."

The doctor paused then nodded. "You're right. I'm sorry."

"Where's Drake?" Evie asked from the bed that the orderlies had just placed her in.

Aiden stepped beside the bed and cupped her cheek. "He's outside. He'll be in as soon as the doctor gives the all clear. As a matter of fact, you have quite a few visitors waiting outside."

She frowned at him. "Piper? Karen?"

"Piper's outside. So is the entire team and their women."

"Uhm-mm," the doctor interrupted.

Evie clutched his arm. "What about Karen?"

"She's fine. I promise. Let me talk to the doctor, okay?"

She gave a small nod.

Chapter Eleven

"I don't like this," Drake said for the forty-first time.

"Would you keep your voice down? Eva is exhausted. She just got to sleep," Aiden said in a low, resigned tone. He was tired, and this conversation was just irritating him.

"She needs to be with family."

"Drake, you can't split your attention. You have to focus on Karen. Evie knows that," Aiden said reasonably.

"Piper can keep an eye on Evie."

"Piper is getting ready to start USD. She needs to concentrate on that. Let me do this."

"She doesn't want to be here." Drake looked around the large living room.

"If she really didn't want to be here, you know she would have dug in her heels. Your sister is ornery. But she acquiesced. She knew this was the right place for her to rest and heal."

Drake sighed. "Yeah. If you fuck this up, I'm going to rip your head off, and-"

"Shit down my neck. I know." Aiden grimaced. "Seriously, you need to come up with new threats."

"So what are you going to do about the two assholes in Tennessee? I promised to leave them up to you, but if you take too long, I'm going to go down there and handle things myself. It's only because you saw her in Turkey that I'm allowing you first dibs." Drake clenched his big fists.

"I want to stay with Evie for a week. Karen should be off bed rest by then, right?"

"How did you know? Oh yeah, medic boy." Drake nodded. "Yeah, six more days. She's already chomping at the bit, but she doesn't want to do anything to endanger Caroline."

Aiden smiled. "What a beautiful name. Caroline Avery. Seriously, man, the docs know what they're doing. She's going to be fine. Anyway, after Karen is off bed rest, I figure you, and she can come over here and stay. I have plenty of room. Then I need twenty-four hours."

"What do you plan?"

"The nuclear option."

"What's that? Explain."

"I'll tell you when I come back. You'll have to trust me."

"Fucking A, she's my sister. I want to know!"

Aiden winced. "Keep it down. I will handle this."

"I want them to bleed." He saw the pain in the big man's black eyes.

"So do I. I'll handle it. You have to trust me. I was there. I carried her out of that room. I'll handle this." Drake stared at him, and finally nodded, apparently satisfied.

"Okay, I'm going to go look in on her one last time."

Aiden shook his head and smiled. He watched him go down the hall, and then went into the kitchen. He needed to start dinner. Hopefully, he could fix something that would tempt Evie. All of the travelling had played havoc on her appetite, and she had hardly touched the food at the hospital, not that he could blame her. He'd called ahead and had his fridge stocked. He pulled out the ingredients to make a pot roast. He knew she liked that.

He looked up when Drake came back out.

"You have all of our numbers?"

Aiden chuckled. "You have to mellow out."

"You sound like a surfer. Has Mason taken you out on the waves?"

"Leave already. I have dinner to cook."

"I'm gone." Drake let himself out the front door, and Aiden breathed a sigh of relief. He finished seasoning the meat, then put it into the pan and into the oven. He washed his hands and made his way down the hall to check on Evie.

She was in the big guest room that was decorated in greens and blues. He'd hoped it would be soothing for her, but looking at the state of the covers, he could see she was having trouble resting. He watched as she rolled over, then he heard her whimper.

God, he didn't want to scare her, but he hated seeing her in distress. He went over and sat on the bed.

"Eva?"

She was murmuring something, but he couldn't make it out. Then she swung her arm out. She was clearly in the middle of a nightmare.

"Oh, Baby. Wake up."

"Stop! Fuck you!" She tried to push up. "Ow!"

Aiden caught her before she hurt herself.

"Get away!" She swung at him, and he gently held her, knowing she was going to hurt her shoulder if he didn't restrain her.

"Eva, wake up. It's me, Aiden. You're safe. You're safe, Kitten. You're safe." Over and over, he continued to talk to her, trying to get through to her. Eventually, she settled.

"Aiden?"

"Yeah, Baby. It's me. Are you with me now?"

She let out a trembling sigh.

"Where am I?"

"You're at my house."

"Where's Drake? Is he still here?"

"He left. He had to get back to Karen. He'll be back tomorrow." Her slight frame relaxed a little more in his arms.

"Karen's okay, right? The baby? I didn't dream that? Everything's been fuzzy."

"You've been through a lot. The surgery, jetlag, and pain killers."

"Kidnapping and beatings," she said with a half-laugh.

"I was getting there," he assured her. "God, you have an amazing spirit." He brushed back her damp hair so he could look into her eyes.

"No, I don't. You're confusing being a smartass with spirit. All I've ever been is a middle sister with a smart mouth." He looked at the mouth in question. Her face was still bruised, but he wanted to kiss her. Needed to kiss her.

He dipped down and slanted his lips ever so softly against her delicate lips. She parted her mouth on a sigh. Where before they had ignited in passion, now they slid into adoration. He cherished the woman in his arms, thankful that he had this chance, but soon the sweet feelings morphed into a tempest of want.

Aiden knew he wasn't alone, because Evie's good arm was wrapped tightly around his neck, but there was no way she was in any condition for anything more than tender kisses. He reached up and unwound her arm.

"No," she protested. "I need this."

"Kitten, you get as many kisses as you want for as long as you want them. But only kisses."

Her nails bit into his shoulder. "I want more. I need this." Then she bit her lip and shook her head as if to clear it.

God, so did he, but she was weeks away from anything physical. What's more, if she had been thinking straight, she would remember she was mad at him. They had too much to resolve before they were intimate. He didn't want to fuck this up. Literally.

"Eva, you're having a reaction to all of your trauma. You want to prove to yourself that you're alive. That you're safe. This is too important. We're too important. In the meantime, I'll kiss you and hold you all you want."

Evie took some deep breaths.

"Maybe you're right."

"I know I am. Do you think you can rest until dinner is ready? Or would you like the TV on?"

"Can I have my laptop?"

Aiden looked at her eyes. The swelling had gone down considerably on her left eye. They had recovered her belongings from the hotel room in Turkey, so she had her laptop there.

"I'll get it for you. But don't strain your eyes, okay?"

"I won't," she assured him.

* * *

Evie heaved a sigh of relief when Aiden left her alone with her laptop and thoughts. What in the hell had gotten into her? Into him? She was a fucking mess. She hurt like a son of a bitch, and she'd been climbing all over him. What the hell? Tears pricked her eyelids. She didn't want this. She didn't need this. She didn't trust him. It had to be the injury. Maybe it was Stockholm syndrome.

She booted up her laptop.

She went to her email. There were two emails each day from Jim, and one a day from Blake. She ignored them. Trenda had sent two today. Drake had said she wanted to fly to California, but Evie knew that money was tight for her. She eyed the landline on the nightstand beside the bed. First, she perused her sister's email.

Dammit. Trenda was already explaining how she intended to cash in one of her hard won IRA's for the flight. It was time to call.

Evie hated making a long distance call on Aiden's phone without asking permission, but she also couldn't get out of bed without a whole hell of a lot of pain. So she was screwed. She picked up the phone and dialed Trenda's number. Thank God, it was one of the two she had memorized.

"Hello?"

"Trenda, it's me, Evie."

"Oh, Baby Girl, it's so good to hear your voice. Drake promised you would call me this morning." Trenda promptly started to cry.

"Hey, hey, hey. I'm fine."

Her sister said something, but she couldn't understand her. She waited until the tears subsided. This wasn't her first rodeo with Trenda. Most of the time she was a rock, but when she lost it, she really lost it.

Finally…

"God, Evie. I'll be there in three days."

"Bullshit. You can't afford it. Did you tell Drake you were cashing an IRA?"

"It's done. The tickets are bought."

"You lie."

"I go in and sign the paperwork tomorrow. It's almost done," Trenda admitted.

"Well stop it. I'm going to ask Aiden to pay. Apparently, he's richer than God." Evie damn near stopped breathing as soon as the words were out of her mouth. She hadn't just said that, had she?

"He is not."

"He is. I'm lying in a bedroom that is bigger than my entire hotel suite. He's loaded. The TV costs more than my car." She looked at the flat screen that took up half the wall. What? He thought his guests needed to have the TV characters join them in bed?

"You can't ask him. You hate him."

Evie blushed and remained silent as she thought about the kiss they had just shared. What in the hell had gotten into her? Oh yeah, Stockholm syndrome. She was definitely going with that. Except, he was her rescuer, so that didn't really fly, now did it?

"Evie? What aren't you telling your big sister? I recognize that guilty silence."

"The man just saved my life. How could I possibly hate him?"

"Not hating him because he saved your life, and moving in with him and borrowing money from him are three different things. Are you being foolish?" Trenda's Southern accent was more pronounced as she got into her mother hen role.

"For God's sake, I'm sick in bed. I just got out of surgery three days ago. How could I have gotten into trouble already?"

"Because you're Evalyn Lavender Avery, that's how. Now spill it."

Evie bit her bottom lip that was still slightly tender from the kiss she had shared with Aiden. God, she needed to talk, but would Trenda judge her? Then she thought about everything that her sister had gone through in her life and knew that she would be the last person in the world to judge.

"Something's changed with him. I feel it. I'm beginning to trust him."

"Of course, something's changed. He almost lost you," Trenda said gently.

"I think it's more than that," Evie persisted. She was met with silence.

"He said he was trying to protect me before."

"What does he mean by that?"

"Fuck if I know."

"Seriously, there are other words besides 'fuck'," Trenda admonished.

Evie hunched over. "I don't say it in front of Bella...much."

"I'm sorry, I shouldn't be lecturing you. You don't know what he meant about protecting you? He didn't elaborate?"

"I fell asleep before he could. Now, he's insisted I stay with him. He's acting like he cares, and not because he kissed me. He's all gentle and loving. He's driving me up a wall. He's even more caring than he was at the chalet back in Tennessee."

"He kissed you?" Trenda's voice rose. At least she didn't screech.

"Please stay calm. I haven't told you the worst part."

She heard Trenda take a deep breath. "Okay, hit me."

"I responded. A lot. I was all over him, like bees to honey."

"Oh, Baby Girl. Do you think it was the pain medicine?"

"I'm voting on Stockholm syndrome."

Trenda shouted with laughter. "Only you."

"He broke it off. God, he was so tender I almost cried."

"Well, he damn well better be tender considering your condition. You need to be wrapped in cotton wool."

"I do not," Evie groused.

"Well, you will be when I fly out there. I'll have enough money to stay close by."

"You are not staying at a hotel. Aiden's house has a bazillion rooms. You are not cashing one of your two IRA's." Evie shoved the receiver against her chest and then winced at the pressure.

"Aiden!" she yelled. She waited.

In less than a minute he was in the doorway, dishtowel in his hands, and a concerned look on his face. Then he saw the phone pressed against her chest and his expression changed to quizzical.

"What's going on."

Time to take the bull by the horns.

"You're rich. Trenda is planning to cash in one of her two IRA's to pay for a ticket for her and Bella to fly out here and stay at a hotel so she can be near me."

He strode into the room and held out his hand for the phone. She handed it to him.

"Trenda?"

He listened to whatever bullshit she was spouting. Finally, he interrupted.

"There will be tickets for you and Bella in your email within the hour. You're staying at my place. I have five bedrooms and six baths."

Evie watched the play of emotions that passed over his face. Finally, he grinned.

"No, I really wasn't planning that many children. I have a large family that comes and visits from Mexico twice a year. They expect to stay with me, I needed the room."

His grin got broader.

"I'll keep that in mind." He thrust the phone back to Evie. "Here, she wants to speak to you. I'll give you some privacy. Anyway, I have potatoes to peel."

He walked back out the door.

"Five bedrooms and six bathrooms?"

"I told you he was Midas rich."

"He has more bathrooms than bedrooms. Who has that?"

"He's got dark hair."

"What?" Trenda asked. "You're not making sense."

"He doesn't look like himself. He has dark hair. He dyed it to blend in while he was in Turkey. I felt like I was kissing someone else. Do you think that was why it was a different kind of kiss? Do you think it was the hair color?" Her toes still curled. She still got fuzzy, and God, every single girl part woke up and took notice. She needed to have her head examined.

"Definitely the pain medicine." Trenda sighed. "I need to get out there stat."

"It was the best kiss of my life," Evie whispered as she smoothed the sheet. Hell, what was the thread count?

"Oh, Honey." Trenda sighed. "Don't get in too deep, okay? You're still coming off a horrific event, and it'd be so easy to fall into his arms because he represents safety. You need to rest and get well. Wait until we get there, okay? You need a sense of normalcy. Once Bella and I are there, all that nonsense will stop."

Maybe Trenda was right. Plus, there was something else she needed to discuss.

"Jim and Blake keep e-mailing me."

"I know, Baby Girl. They keep calling me. Blake stopped by. I didn't answer the door. If I had, I would have slapped him. Don't even open the e-mails."

"They helped rescue me."

"They're the ones that put you in that situation, to begin with. They are the bad guys. Don't open. I don't want you feeling bad for them. Are we clear?"

"But-"

"Don't 'but' me."

Evie looked down at the e-mails. It seemed like their names were glowing large on the screen.

"Delete them. Delete them right now while I'm on the phone."

"But we have so much history. Jim and Blake have been so good to me." She continued to stare at the screen. Then a large hand plucked her computer off her laptop.

"What the fuck?"

"Those assholes are trying to get ahold of you?" Aiden roared.

He had her laptop cradled in his right hand, and he scrolled through her emails.

"That's private."

"It isn't now. I can't believe this."

"Are you clicking on those?"

"Damn right I am." He didn't say anything. His expression was glacial, his blue eyes glittered like ice chips.

"What, what did they say?"

She watched as he pressed keys.

"Dammit, are you deleting those?"

"Yes," he bit out. "This is trash. They are trying to salve their conscience."

"Of course they are. They feel bad. I was going to open them eventually," Evie explained.

"You are never going to talk to them again. They are dead to you."

She looked at him as if he had grown a second head. "Handsome, the hair dye has rotted your brain. You are not going to dictate who I do, and who I don't, talk to."

"Dead."

"Jim made a dumb fucking decision. He's got to live with that. It's going to haunt him for the rest of his life. That's punishment enough."

"No, it isn't."

Trenda's "Amen," could be heard through the phone. Evie put the receiver back up to her ear.

"I have a situation going on here, Sis. I'll call you back."

"Remind her to look for the tickets."

"Tell him I heard him," Trenda said.

"I've got to go and talk to the high-handed bastard."

"I'm beginning to like him again."

"Good-bye, Trenda." Evie hung up the phone and glared up at Aiden who looked at her unrepentantly.

"Give me back my laptop."

He walked across the room and set it on the dresser. She watched as he scrolled through her in-box and continued to delete e-mails. "You get a lot of spam. You need a better filter."

Evie pushed up on the bed.

"I see you, don't you dare try to get out of that bed."

"You don't have eyes in the back of your head," she protested.

He pointed to the window. She saw that her image was reflected on it. She slumped down against the pillows.

"Give. Me. My. Laptop."

"Okay." He strolled back and handed her the computer. She noted that all emails from Blake and Jim were gone, and her trash deleted.

Dammit!

"You're annoying."

He pulled out his wallet. He took out a credit card and his driver's license. "Book Trenda and Bella a flight. Make it first class."

"I am not going to book a first class ticket. That would just freak her out."

He raised an eyebrow. "Think of it as retribution for me deleting your emails."

She flicked his cards between her fingers and slowly grinned. "You do deserve to be punished."

"By the time you're done booking the reservations, dinner will be ready."

"I'm not all that hungry."

"You'll eat," he said in a low voice.

"Bossy."

"It comes with the job." He left her, and she spent long minutes finding the best prices, but she did book them first class seats. It was pretty damned exciting. She would have loved to see Trenda's face when she flew first class. She forwarded the reservations to her sister's email. Within five minutes the phone beside her was ringing but she ignored it. Let Aiden deal with it.

Evie had given up on her laptop and turned on the TV after Aiden left. She was still going through the myriad of cable channels when he came in carrying a tray of food. It smelled delicious.

"Did you make pot roast?"

"It won't be as good as yours," he warned.

"You made pot roast." She grinned and turned off the TV. He set the tray on her lap.

She picked up her fork and scooped up some mashed potatoes. "These are homemade."

"I told you I was peeling potatoes."

"You made homemade mashed potatoes and pot roast." She looked up at him, her eyes shining.

"You made the same for me the first night we were at the chalet. I thought you would like it."

Evie cut a slice of roast and found she could have used her fork it was so succulent. She took a bite. "Oh Aiden, this is delicious." She watched as he smiled. "Are you going to join me?"

"I was planning to, but first I wanted to make sure you were going to actually eat. I had my doubts."

"I thought you expected to be obeyed," she teased.

"You aren't always that easy."

She took another bite, then waved her fork at him. "You better hurry before I'm done."

"Don't forget to eat your vegetables and drink your milk."

Evie rolled her eyes as he left the room. Soon he was back with another tray. He came around to the other side of the bed and made himself comfortable beside her. What had seemed like a huge bed just moments ago now seemed tiny. The man was gigantic.

"What?"

"You have big feet," she said pointing to his feet. "All of you is big."

"If you drink your milk, maybe you'll grow an inch or two and not feel so intimidated by people's size."

She looked at the heaping amounts of food on his plate. Already, she was getting full.

"Eva, don't you like the food? I thought this was one of your favorite meals." He took another bite. Then he picked up a spear of asparagus and waved it in front of her face. "Come on this will make you strong. I sautéed it in butter. Lots of butter. Even you should like it."

"What do you mean, even me?"

"I mean that if you don't use a stick of butter with every meal you cook, then you think something is wrong. I swear to God, those grits you kept making were a third butter, a third sugar, and a third paste."

"Yeah, but that way everybody eats them." She gave him a sideways smile.

He waggled the asparagus again. She plucked it from his fingers and delicately bit into the tip. She hummed. "Oh, my God, this is delicious."

"Butter." He smiled. Then he picked one up and ate it.

"So did I start you down the road to ruin?"

"No, I still eat my food steamed. This is just an indulgence for you."

Evie felt her heart melt. She took a sip of milk so he wouldn't notice her features going all soft and gooey. She could only take a couple of sips. She really was getting full. He must have noticed, because he didn't try to push any more food on her. Instead, he pretended to focus on his meal, but she knew he was still aware of her. It was kind of nice and annoying at the same time.

"Stop it."

"Stop what?" he asked.

"You're examining me like I'm going to fall apart at any minute. I'm not. You rescued me. I'm back in America. I just got to eat pot roast. I'm good." She even managed a bright smile.

"Eva, I think it's time for some pain medicine. You look pale."

"See! You were watching me. I'm not some kind of bug."

Aiden set down his fork, got up, put his tray on the dresser, then came around and got hers as well. "How bad is the pain?"

She hated to admit it, but it was bad.

"On a level of one to ten," he asked.

"Four," she answered.

"So a seven. I'll be right back with your meds."

She stuck her tongue out at his retreating back. The damned irritating man was right, she really hurt. She pressed her hand against her abdomen, then against her shoulder.

"Suck it up, buttercup. You're safe. It could have been much worse."

She closed her eyes, and a fist came flying at her. She jerked across the bed.

"Eva! Baby!"

"No! Please!" She scuttled further away, hands grabbed at her, and she screamed. It took her a long moment to realize that she didn't feel cement under her, she felt something soft. The hands weren't hurting.

"Shhhh, Eva, you're safe. You're safe."

She wasn't being held down, she was being stroked. These arms felt familiar and good.

Evie shuddered. She took in Aiden's scent, and it was what finally calmed her. She burrowed in, and shoved her face against his neck. He rubbed his big hand up and down the length of her spine, and she slowly came back to herself.

The present.

She was in San Diego. She wasn't in that room. Nobody was going to hurt her.

"Nobody's going to hurt you, Baby, I've got you."

She took a deep breath. Another. Then another. She tried to push out of his arms, but he wouldn't let her go. She liked it. She didn't really want to leave. Every little bit of strength left her, and she melted against him. But then she started to shiver. To shudder.

Oh, God. Not tears. There was never any point to crying. Her eyes started to sting, and then…and then.

"I don't want to cry."

He kissed the top of her head.

"I know you don't," he whispered into her hair. Tears started. She tried to pull away from him so he wouldn't feel them. He cupped her nape and held her close to the crook of his neck. "I won't tell anyone you cried."

Ahhh, God, he'd said the wrong thing.

Tears started to flow, big fat ones. Gushing. Sobbing.

"Let the poison out."

"I was…" She gulped. "I was scared." She clutched at Aiden, as she tried to get closer, if she could have, she would have climbed into his skin.

He rocked her back and forth.

"I have you. You're safe. I have you now."

The more he said it, the more she embraced her fear and let it go. It was as if she could face it in the haven of his arms.

Evie cried. And cried. And cried.

After forever, she felt his thumbs brushing the tears off her cheeks, his lips at her temple, his voice in her mind. "You're safe. I have you."

Sleep came.

* * *

He couldn't let her go. He crawled into bed beside her, and she clutched him even closer. Aiden stared at the large stain of water on the carpet, where he'd dropped the glass when he'd come in the room with her pain meds. He'd been waiting for her to break down, but he'd still been taken by surprise.

She was too warm from her crying, but that wasn't going to stop him from holding her close. He reached across her and picked up the remote for the fan and turned it on high.

Aiden gave a heavy sigh. Every time Evie had said she'd been scared, he'd thought the same thing. He'd been terrified. He just couldn't let it hamper his ability to focus. But Jesus, he'd been scared. Hell, not even at fifteen when he'd gone after the gang members who'd raped and killed his mother had he felt such fear. Knowing Evie was being held and tortured had ripped at his soul.

She nuzzled against his chest. He looked down at her delicate features. Had he really thought it was possible to let her go? God, he'd been stupid. Yeah, he'd thought that he still had people out after him, and he was doing it to protect her, but life was just too fucking short. It shouldn't have mattered.

He cupped her head and pressed her cheek to his heart.

"Rest Eva, I have you. I have you."

Chapter Twelve

Evie looked at Aiden out of the corner of her eye. She was in the living room, finally off bed rest, thank the Lord. She would have thought that he would go insane with having his home overrun with Averys, but he seemed perfectly relaxed. No, the only person who seemed tense was her big brother.

Scratch that, Karen was out of sorts too, but that was only because she was a nanosecond away from killing Drake. Seriously, if he offered to do one more thing for her, he was going to get hit.

"Karen, would you like a bottle of water?"

"Sure, it would go well with the one I'm holding, Sweetheart." She smiled at her big fiancé.

Trenda laughed, then Bella giggled. "Why are we laughing, Mommy?"

"Because your uncle is a worrywart," Karen answered for Trenda.

Bella got up off the floor where she was coloring and toddled over to the couch where Karen was sitting. "What's a working wart?"

"Uncle Drake is working to get warts at the rate he's going," Evie told Bella. Evie watched Bella reach out to stroke Karen's stomach. Before Drake could lose his mind, she walked over to pick up her niece. Somehow, like Flash Gordon, Aiden was by her side and picked up Bella.

"Eva, you're not supposed to be picking up anything more than five pounds for a few weeks yet."

Bella patted Aiden's cheek. "O-Man! Higher!" He accommodated by swinging her up toward the ceiling. She shrieked with laughter.

"Do you want another bottle of water, Karen?" Evie asked sweetly.

"I think you should try to go and lift something, *Eva*," the woman responded sarcastically. Evie sighed. Karen was right. They were surrounded by vigilant men.

"Evie, you knew better than to pick up Bella," Trenda admonished.

She bowed her head. Her sister was right. "Sorry, Trenda. I wasn't thinking."

Trenda picked up the coloring book and crayons, and came over and put her arm around Evie. "It's okay. I just worry about you."

"We all do," Piper said from her seat near the window.

"I'm fine."

"You're getting there," Trenda said. "Don't try to push it."

"Don't you need to worry about Karen?" she said hopefully.

"Nah, Drake has that covered," Trenda said tongue in cheek.

"Gee, thanks, Trenda," Karen said.

Evie looked at her soon-to-be sister-in-law. She looked beautiful. Her red hair gleamed, and her green eyes sparkled. There was no way that Evie would have thought that there was anything wrong with her. Just then, she moved her hands over the curve of her protruding stomach, and a shadow passed over her face as she bit her lip. Drake had been looking up at Bella, but almost as is if he had a psychic connection to Karen, he turned and caught her chin between his fingers and gave her a gentle kiss.

"How's Miss Caroline?" he asked.

"She just kicked."

"Well of course she did. She knows Bella is having fun, and she wants to join in," he teased. Just like that, Karen relaxed. Maybe vigilant was a good thing.

"How does it feel to know you're going to continue to be surrounded by women?" Evie asked her big brother.

He put his arm around Karen and leaned against the sofa. "I can't imagine anything better."

Evie glanced over at Trenda, who was looking as happy as she was feeling. God, after everything he had gone through, it was damn fine to see their big brother so happy. Nobody deserved it more.

"What?" Drake looked between the two of them.

"Never you mind," Karen said, as she handed him her empty water bottle. "I need a refill big guy."

Boy, she sure knew how to work him.

She winked at Evie as Drake got up to get her another bottle of water. Aiden cuddled Bella close, then placed her gently on the floor next to Trenda. "I'm going to go out and get your stuff out of the car."

"Whose stuff?" Evie asked.

"Karen, Piper, and Drake are staying here for the next two days," Aiden said casually. Too casually.

She looked at Karen, who shrugged. "Drake's tried to keep me in the dark, then fed me some stupid story. Consider me a mushroom. He's been shoveling bullshit."

"Auntie Karen said a bad word," Bella whispered to her mother.

Trenda sighed, and Karen laughed.

"Bella, Uncle Drake owes you money, because he's responsible for my bad word. Go ask him for your money."

Drake walked into the living room holding two bottles of water. "What money?" he asked.

"I said a swear word and it's your fault. You owe your niece some cash."

"Why is that my fault," he asked as he twisted the cap off the water and handed it to Karen.

"Because you're covering me in B.S. What are you and Aiden up to? Why do we need to spend the next two nights here? Where is Aiden going?"

Evie's felt her pulse speed up. *Calm down, girl!* It's not a big deal that Aiden won't be here.

"Where's Aiden going?" she asked casually.

"He didn't tell you?" Drake asked innocently.

The front door opened and Aiden came in with two suitcases and a duffle bag.

"Thanks, man," Drake said.

Aiden tipped his chin. "I'm putting them in the room across from Trenda and Bella's. The smaller room next to it is for Piper."

"Did you decorate this house?" Piper asked.

Aiden chuckled. "Heck no," he said as he grinned at Bella who was listening to the adult's conversation. "My aunt and uncle got sick of staying at the Hyatt when they came and visit. Uncle Leonard scoped out the house and insisted I buy it. Aunt Carmen made a trip from the Yucatan, and had this decorated in two weeks. I didn't have to lift a finger." He headed down the hall with the luggage.

"I'll help with the suitcases," Evie said as she got up out of her chair, "you might need help lifting something." She caught up with him as he dropped the luggage on the bed.

"Where are you going? Why didn't you tell me you were leaving? Are you being deployed? I thought you were still on leave."

He gently cupped her shoulders. The man was always conscious of her injuries. She hated that she was still sore. Dammit.

"I was going to tell you, Evie."

"When? When you got back?"

"If I thought I could have gotten away with it, yeah." He smiled down at her. She liked that he was back to being a blond again. Then again, maybe not. Now he could say almost anything, and she would just go along with it.

"Don't think you're going to get away with a damn thing just because you're handsome. That might work with all of your women, but I'm your roommate. You need to keep me informed."

"Roommate, huh?" His fingertips slowly slid down the back of her arms, until he was holding her elbows. Then he trailed them down further until they tangled with hers. She clutched his hands.

"How are you feeling? You know if Bella comes down with something, as kids are prone to do, she and Trenda will have to go stay at the Hyatt, right? You're susceptible to infection."

"Don't try to change the subject, Mr. Medic. Where are you going?"

"I'll be back soon. I'm just going to be going to gone two nights, max. I'm going to call you each night. We'll talk until you go to sleep."

Her fingers tightened. She had nightmares. He knew she did. Almost every night he ended up coming into her room and holding her until he chased the shadows away. The first three nights before Trenda arrived, he came running in when she'd wake up screaming. She thought about the first night after her sister's arrival. He waited for everyone to settle in, then he showed up in her room wearing sweatpants with a book and settled in beside her.

"I've decided I won't dream tonight," she'd assured him.

"Good, it would interrupt my reading."

"The light's going to bother me."

"Close your eyes, then you won't notice it."

She rolled over and finally slept. At some point, she remembered waking up scared, but was soon soothed by Aiden's familiar scent and calming voice promising her safety. She'd fallen back to sleep.

"Kitten, it's important. I'm pretty sure I'll be back tomorrow."

"It's not a problem. You know the dreams are getting better." And they had been.

He pressed his forehead against hers, and looked into her eyes. "I know. I'm so impressed with you. I don't know how you've managed to fight your way out of this like you have."

"It's what you would do."

"I still think you should talk to someone."

"I never have before."

Fuck! She hadn't meant to say that. She slid her eyes away from his.

"Eva. Look at me."

She got lost in royal blue. His eyes were dark with compassion. "Have you been holding out on me?"

"Where are you going?"

"Have you been holding out on me? What else has happened to you?"

"I asked you first. Where are you going?"

His eyes searched hers.

"I'm going to Tennessee."

Evie tried to step back, but he wouldn't let her. "Careful, Eva, you're still healing," he warned her.

"Why are you going to Jasper Creek?"

"Blake and Jim have continued to email you. It needs to stop."

"No, they haven't." She checked her email daily, and there hadn't been any emails from either of them. Part of her had been relieved, but a larger part of her had been hurt.

"I had them forwarded to my email. Dex did it."

"Dex? He's the tech guy who helped to rescue me. You arranged to have him hijack my email? What the fuck?!" She tried to twist out of his hold, but he gathered her gently against his chest.

"Calm down. I didn't want them trying to assuage their guilt. They have no right."

"No, you have no right!"

"I will not have you upset. You're still healing. I will do everything in my power to make sure you are taken care of."

"That's utter bullshit. I take care of myself. I always take care of myself." As soon as the words were out of her mouth, she realized just what a lie they were. She'd been letting him take care of her for the last week. It had to stop. She shouldn't allow herself to come to rely on him. "Let me go," she said as she pulled out of his arms.

She ran across the hall to her room, unsurprised that he followed her.

"Eva, I didn't mean to upset you."

She took three deep breaths. She would not throw herself across the bed and cry like she wanted to. She turned to look at Aiden.

"What are you going to say to Jim and Blake?"

"I'm going to tell them to cease and desist."

No, he wasn't. She knew him now. He wasn't pissed. He wasn't angry the way that Drake got angry, he was ice. He was going to go obliterate them. "What are you going to do?"

"I haven't decided, but I can promise you I'm not going to kill them."

Evie laughed. He stared at her. She stopped laughing.

"You can't be serious."

"It was a consideration. At least with Jim."

"You can't kill a man in cold blood."

"It's been done a time or two."

"Not by you."

"It's been done a time or two," he said quietly. She looked at him. Really looked at him. Holy fuck, she didn't think he was kidding.

"I'm going to make it fast, Eva. I'll be back tomorrow. I won't prolong this. Okay? Now answer my question."

What was he talking about? Did he just say he'd killed someone in cold blood? "What question?"

"Has something like the kidnapping and beating happened to you in the past?"

Evie sucked in a deep breath. She took a step backward, and he took a step forward. She lifted her arms to ward him off and winced.

"Dammit, be careful." He gently grasped her injured arm and pulled it down to relieve the pressure.

"Eva, you can trust me. I would never hurt you."

"Oh, God, Aiden, of course, you wouldn't. I know that."

"Then what?"

She took a deep breath and gave a half smile. "Sounds like both of us still have some skeletons in our closets. You come back from Tennessee. Hopefully, you won't have any blood on your hands. Then we'll swap some stories."

"I want you to talk to me now."

She wasn't going to just dance to his tune. "How come I don't know anything about your childhood."

He flinched. Direct hit.

"You sure you want to go there?" he asked.

"We missed a few steps before. You keep saying we have a chance. You say you want something with me. Well, it's time to go a little bit below the surface, don't you think?" She held her breath to see what he'd say.

He held out his hands. She put hers in his. He brought them up to his lips and turned them over. He kissed her palms. "Deal."

CHAPTER THIRTEEN

Driving up to the boutique hotel, he saw that all of the contractor's trucks were gone, and instead, there were mostly rental cars in the parking lot. Now wasn't that just nice for two men who had almost gotten a woman killed, Aiden thought bitterly.

He parked away from the rest of the vehicles, underneath a copse of trees, and took advantage of the walk to center himself. Aiden knew what he wanted to accomplish, and it shouldn't take long.

He walked up the flower-lined flagstone stairs leading to the entrance.

"Can I help you? Do you have a reservation?" The young girl behind the desk was pretty and chipper.

"I'm here to visit with Mr. Sellers."

"Is he expecting you?" she asked with a head tilt.

"No, but he'll see me. Tell him that Aiden O'Malley is here." Aiden was careful to stay back from the desk, not wanting to tower over the lone female in the lobby. She lifted the phone and spoke quietly.

"He'll be out directly." She pointed to the coffee station. "Help yourself." She smiled.

Aiden shook his head.

Jim came out from the back office.

"How's Evie?" he asked as soon as he saw Aiden. The man looked haggard. Good.

Aiden tilted his head toward the entrance door and opened it. Jim walked through it.

"Let's take a walk."

As soon as they got outside, Jim glanced sideways at him. "A dead body in the forest is going to be noticed," Jim said, only half joking.

"I'm not going to kill you," Aiden replied as they headed out behind the hotel toward the tree line.

"You considered it though."

"Drake did."

Jim's step faltered. It was clear that the former Army Ranger had been out of the game for too damn long. Still, Aiden had no pity.

"All I ask is that you keep Blake out of it."

"That's up to you."

The leaves from the trees muted their footsteps as they started up an incline. When they were finally out of sight of the hotel, Aiden stopped.

"Do your worst." Jim's expression was resigned.

"I don't want Evie to have any reminders of Turkey."

"Neither do I." Jim spread his hands apart and gave Aiden a look of relief. "Neither does Blake. God, we would do anything to erase those days from Evie's memory."

"You can't. She dreams about them every night."

The man winced like he'd taken a hit. "Fuck. I'm so fucking sorry. I should have never tried to help Nathan."

Aiden looked at him incredulously. "That wasn't your error. You're a Ranger for God's sake, you're supposed to be trained to think. Why would you have taken an innocent into a potentially dangerous situation?"

"Antakya is such a historic city, and I didn't want to cut Evie's vacation short."

"What about Blake? Did you give two shits about him? Your buddy was asking for thirty large in cash, and you just danced right into the situation with two people you say you love."

Jim blanched.

"You need to get gone."

"I don't understand. That's it? You just wanted to say that to me?"

Aiden strove for his center. "No, you stupid ass. You need to pull up stakes and leave Tennessee. Gone. Out of town. Into the wind. You have a week."

Jim opened his mouth to say something. His throat worked, but no words came out. He stood there with his mouth open, struggling for something to say. He got red in the face, finally saying, "you have no right."

"You don't deserve to breathe the same air as Evie. This is her home. This is where she grew up. This is where her sisters live. You leave." Aiden's tone was deadly.

"You don't have any right to tell us what to do," he repeated.

"Maybe. But I'm telling you anyway. One week. I'll be checking on you. Next Tuesday, you're gone. Don't step back in Tennessee for one goddamned reason after that. You disappear. I don't want Evie to be able to get ahold of you. I want all traces of you gone. I want your numbers changed. I want you gone. Am I clear?"

Jim's eyes turned beady. "Make me."

"This way I'm leaving you with money for a new stake."

"Make me."

"I'll bury you."

"They'll figure out you murdered me. Try it."

"I mean I'll strip you of everything you own, then I'll really come after you. You think it was slick how we got that story planted about the corpse? Imagine the things we can make up about you? Imagine what the cops will come knocking on your door for? Identity theft will look like your wildest dream come true by the time we're done with you."

"I'll go to the authorities."

Aiden smiled. "By all means, please do." He watched with satisfaction as he saw Jim's fist clench. Please, God, say the man was truly that stupid. Jim stepped forward and swung.

Aiden stepped to the side, and rabbit punched him twice in the spleen. Jim grunted but stayed on his feet. He backed up and looked at Aiden, then his foot shot out, Aiden twisted out of the way and yanked Jim's arm down as he took him to the ground and rolled. He heard a satisfying pop as Jim's shoulder dislocated.

Jim continued to roll as Aiden got off the ground. Kicking a man while he was down had never been so satisfying. He really didn't give a shit if he broke a rib or two as he plowed his boot into Jim's ribcage.

Out of the corner of his eye, he saw movement at the tree line. It was Blake. He stepped away from Jim.

"I heard we had a visitor," Blake said as he helped his partner off the ground. "I figured it would be either your or Drake. I had my money on you."

"He wants us to leave everything and get the hell out of Tennessee," Jim said bitterly.

Blake looked at Jim, then at Aiden, quietly assessing both of them. "Then we leave."

"You don't understand, he wants us to sell the hotel, and be gone by next Tuesday. This is our home. We've put our hearts and souls into this place."

Blake put his arm around Jim's shoulder, offering the man both physical and moral support.

"This was Evie's home first, this will be Evie's home last. He's right, we need to leave," Blake agreed. He looked over at Aiden. "We'll be gone. If the time is ever right, can you tell Evie I love her? I am so sorry for all of this."

Aiden heard the subtext. He was distancing himself from Jim. He wondered if their relationship would endure this. He didn't really care. Aiden nodded to Blake and headed back to his rental car.

* * *

Aiden had called. She'd pretended to fall asleep, and eventually, he'd hung up. Then she'd turned on the TV. She was too afraid that she would end up having a nightmare and start yelling and wake everybody. She was tired and bored. Even making fun of late night commercials was getting old.

She watched as the pretty blonde offered the most spectacular product ever invented that was sure to make her pretty, younger, stronger, *and* it would chop vegetables in record time. She had to buy it *now* because there were only *three* left. But if she acted *now*, she could get *two* for the price of *one*. It was *amazing*!

The sad part was Evie was thinking about calling.

She pushed back the covers and winced. Shit, shouldn't she be done hurting by now? She sighed. She knew she wouldn't. The docs had said the pain would probably continue for three to four weeks. Dammit, she didn't want to take pain medicine.

If anything, it made her more maudlin. She hated getting all emotional. She was gooey enough as is. She should be past this by now. She looked over at the nightstand at the two empty bottles of water. Two a.m. seemed like the perfect time for a kitchen run.

She walked down the shadowed hallway, knowing the way, and didn't see Drake until she was almost on top of him. She cried out.

"Evie, it's me, Drake," he said holding up his hands.

"Goddammit, you scared the piss out of me."

"Oh, Honey, I'm sorry, I should have turned on the light. I wasn't thinking."

She sagged weakly, and he caught her up in his arms.

"You can't sleep either?" he asked.

She shook her head against his chest.

"Come on, let's rustle up some food."

"I'm not hungry, I was coming for some water."

He flipped on the light switch in the kitchen and eyed her critically. "Is it time for some pain meds?"

She grimaced.

"I'll take that as a yes."

"Go get them, and I'll get you some water and food. It's better to take them with food, isn't it?"

"Yes," she reluctantly admitted.

"Dammit, you need a keeper."

"What is with you guys, is it in the SEAL handbook that you've got to be bossy and dictatorial?"

"March into your room, get your pill bottle so I can read the instructions, then sit your happy ass down and eat the food I put in front of you. How's that for bossy and dictatorial?" His eyes twinkled, and she grinned.

"You still haven't told me why you're up."

"You do what I tell you to do, and I'll tell you why I'm up."

"Fine." She turned too quickly to go back down the hallway and ended up grabbing her side.

"Slowly, Sis."

"I'm good," she assured him.

"I know you are, but I worry about you. So take it slow, okay?"

She looked over her shoulder and gave him a wan smile. "Okay."

By the time she was back in the kitchen, he was scrambling eggs.

"I'd fry bacon, but then everybody would smell it and get up. So we're having eggs and cheese on toast."

God, that sounded yummy.

"Now give me your pill bottle, so I can read the instructions."

"You're kidding, right?"

"Nope."

She didn't hand it over. Because, like, for real?

He held out his big hand.

"Drake, this is stupid. You're right, I need food, okay."

He just kept his hand out. Finally, she relented.

"You keep this up, and Karen's not going to marry you."

"I have talents."

"Gah! I don't want to know." She covered her ears. But she watched him as he read the directions and shook the bottle.

"Shit, you're hardly taking any of these. You know if you stay in pain, that's not any good either. You're probably not sleeping at night. Are you always roaming the halls?"

She blushed.

"Evie?"

"Shouldn't you be cooking the eggs? I'm hungry."

He gave her one more serious look, then turned back toward the stove.

She watched as he easily cooked the cheesy eggs and took the toast out of the toaster and buttered it. He plated the food and placed it in front of her. They sat across from one another at the kitchen island.

"Eat."

"Yes, Sir." She saluted.

"I'm not an officer, no saluting."

He took out two tablets and poured some water. "Now take these."

"I only need one."

"It said one or two. You're wincing all over the place. You're in a lot of pain. Now take them both."

She stared at him. He wasn't being dictatorial, he looked genuinely concerned and upset. Just like when he'd been dealing with Karen.

"I'm not fragile, you know."

He reached out, picked up her hand, opened her palm and put the tablets in them. "Take the fucking pills," he growled.

She put the pills in her mouth and took a long sip of water. Hopefully, she would be able to sleep. Otherwise, she would be ordering a vegetable slicer that probably wouldn't make her prettier.

"Now eat." He waved at the plate.

She was halfway through her food when she noticed that he had hardly touched his.

"Drake what's wrong. Is it Karen? The baby?"

"Huh?"

"You're not eating, something bad must be going on."

"Guess that's a giveaway." He ran his hand through his hair, messing it up even more.

"Seriously, what's wrong? You're freaking me out."

He leaned across the island. "I'm so sorry I wasn't there for you, Evie. Can you ever forgive me?"

"What? What did you say?" Evie set down her fork. She must have misunderstood him.

"I wasn't in Turkey."

"You're kidding, right?"

"He came around to the other side of the kitchen counter where she was sitting. He sat down on the barstool next to hers and cupped her face. "I had nightmares. It killed me not being there."

"You had to be here with Karen and your baby," she protested.

His face was anguished. "I know, and it killed me not being there to help you, too."

"But you made sure I was safe. You sent Aiden."

Drake laughed dryly. "I didn't send him, Sis. We almost came to blows when he insisted on going. Nothing was going to stop him from getting to you. That man cares about you. A lot."

"I hope so." She was feeling kind of muzzy. "Drake?"

"What, Honey?"

"Thank you for being you. You're the best big brother a sister could ever hope to have."

"Oh, God, those pills have really gone to your head." He stood up and helped her off the stool. "Let's get you back to bed.

"I'm serious. I know I don't say that, but all of us feel that way. I'm sorry I never said it."

"Evalyn Lavender, you're one special woman, and I'm honored to have you as a sister."

She started to mist up, but luckily a yawn stopped her from falling apart. "Okay, no more mushy stuff. I need to go to bed."

"I love you, Sis."

"Back at you."

Drake laughed as he guided her down the hall.

"Aiden has his hands full."

"Damn right he does."

Chapter Fourteen

Evie was waiting at the end of the driveway when Aiden pulled up. He sighed. She had her arms crossed, and if she were feeling better, he would bet she would be tapping her foot. He got out of the car.

"Shouldn't you be inside?"

"I wanted to have this discussion outside. Leslie called me." He assumed Leslie was the girl at the front desk at the hotel.

"And?"

"Jim was supposedly in a car wreck, and he and Blake are short selling the hotel. So tell me what you've done."

"Let's go inside." He put his arm around her shoulders, still careful of the one that was tender. She shrugged him off.

"Answer my question."

"I told them they had to leave town."

"You had no right."

"God, you sound like Jim." He put his hand on her lower back and gave a gentle push towards the house. This time she started toward it.

"Well, we're both correct. What gave you the nerve?"

"Did you want to see Jim?"

She stopped dead in her tracks. "Eventually."

"I'll take that as a 'No.'"

"I said eventually," she protested.

"Eva, you deserve to go to Jasper Creek and rest easy that you won't run into the men who sold you out."

She turned and put her hands on Aiden's hard chest. "They didn't sell me out. Jim didn't mean for that to happen. He made a mistake."

"A mistake he was trained not to make."

"Aiden. Call them back."

"No."

"Then I will."

"Go ahead," he smiled coolly. They better have changed their numbers by now.

"They won't listen to me, will they."

"Not if they value their lives."

She stared up at him. "What would you do to them if they didn't leave?"

"I wouldn't kill them if that's what you're worried about. But they know the alternative. They chose to leave, Eva. Let's leave it at that, okay?"

"I can't change your mind?"

"We need to get you inside. The doctor said only mild activity for a while." She was so full of fire, but he saw the lines of strain around her eyes and mouth. "I worry about you."

"Dammit, Aiden, do you have to be so protective all the damn time? I want to stay mad at you."

He grinned. He *was* making headway.

* * *

Evie absolutely adored Trenda and Bella, but she wished they were on the other side of the planet. Aiden had gotten back three hours ago. Karen, Drake, and Piper had promptly left which she so appreciated, but Trenda had made dinner, and they were all eating and quietly laughing at Bella's attempts to mimic the adults.

"Honey, why don't I cut your spaghetti?" Evie suggested.

"I want to whirl it."

Spaghetti sauce splattered across the table as the little girl attempted to twirl the pasta around her fork.

"Isabella, let your aunt cut your spaghetti," Trenda said firmly.

"No!" she said as she quickly stuffed a huge forkful into her mouth. Evie spared a glance at Aiden. He had his napkin over his mouth so Bella couldn't see him laugh. As much as she liked seeing the man smile, she wanted her alone time with him. Surreptitiously, she looked at the watch on his wrist. At least two more hours before Bella's bedtime, and five more before Trenda would go to bed.

Damn, damn, damn.

"Bella, you've earned a timeout."

Evie's head shot up. Bella hardly ever earned a timeout. But then again, she had been acting a little brattish. Evie looked over to see her twirling more pasta. Hell, no wonder Trenda was getting pissed.

"No."

"Oh yes. If you're not careful, there will be no TV for you tomorrow morning."

Bella dropped her fork with a clatter and stared mutinously at her mother.

"Apologize for making a mess."

Bella crossed her arms.

"Isabella," her mother said, the warning clear.

She looked up through thick lashes to Aiden. "Sorry."

"It's bath time." Trenda went over and picked up her daughter. "I'll come out later and clean up."

"I've got it," Evie assured her.

"You're still resting."

"I've got the dishes," Aiden said easily.

"She's angry Piper had to leave. They were playing dress-up," Trenda explained.

"Am not," Bella interrupted.

"Don't push it, little girl. I'll take away your TV privileges." The two females stared at one another. Evie almost smiled. God, they looked so much alike, but Bella hadn't inherited her sister's easy disposition.

"I think I'll call it a night. Missy needs to go to bed early. I need to catch up on some work. There are some logos I'm still fiddling with." Trenda headed down the hallway. "Goodnight."

"Goodnight, Trenda," Aiden said.

"Night," Evie called out.

As soon as they heard the door shut, Aiden started to chuckle. "My God, she's just like you."

"Huh?"

"The way she can get her tail in a twist and act out. God, when she crossed her arms, I thought I was going to lose it. Thank God she's against swearing. Otherwise, she'd grow up to be a carbon copy of you."

"Are you saying I'm a four-year-old?"

Aiden eyed her. "Trust me, there is nothing childlike about you." His tone was low and seductive. "What I am saying is that your niece is going to grow up to be just like her aunt."

"We're nothing alike, she's so happy and vibrant."

Aiden put his napkin down on the table and gave her an incredulous look. "Eva, you are so full of life. My God, you shine."

"Yeah sure. I'm a hot mess, always have been. I'm surly and rude."

"You don't see yourself at all, do you? Everybody lights up when you're around. They want to please you."

"Because they're scared of me."

"Because they look up to you, and they want to have you smile at them. You have a gorgeous smile. Hell, I'm just speaking for myself, but I live for those moments when you look up at me through your lashes and give me a sly smile like Bella. Then there are your grins. When you laugh, hell, that just brightens a room."

Evie's eyes got wide at the way he was describing her. Nobody had ever said anything close to that. Her one and only boyfriend had said she was moody and scary.

"What's going on in that head of yours?"

"I'm not moody and scary?"

"Well, sometimes you're scary. But I like it. Keeps me on my toes."

This was way too much to handle. He hadn't been kidding, he really liked her. She picked up her plate and glass and headed to the kitchen. He followed her.

"So, are you going to tell me about your trip to Tennessee?"

"After the dishes are done. How are you feeling?"

"Pretty good. I should be able to go home soon."

"Hmmmm, we'll see about that," he said as he opened the dishwasher. "Why don't you head to the living room. I'll be out in a minute."

She went directly to the big plate glass window. Over the tree tops, she could see a little bit of the ocean. The sun was setting, and it was gorgeous. Big gentle hands slid down her arms, and she leaned against Aiden's chest. They stood that way until the sun slid beneath the ocean.

"You're lucky, this is a beautiful view. Did you always live in houses like this?"

"Not hardly. We had a two-room house in Chicago where I grew up. Dad was a cop, mom was a housewife. It was exactly like they wanted it."

"How do your aunt and uncle fit into the picture?"

"Uncle Leonard was my mom's cousin, but he was like a brother to her. He was pissed that she wouldn't have anything to do with the family's money. But their business in Veracruz was shady, to say the least."

"Your dad must have loved that," she said wryly.

"Not so much."

"Uncle Leonard has made it legit in recent years, but that was after Dad died. I didn't have any contact with the Canul side of the family growing up."

"What about your mom's parents?"

"She was orphaned when she was a child. She was raised by Leonard's parents. That's why they were so close. It really was a blow when she turned her back on them and clung to my dad."

"So you're mostly an O'Malley."

"I was. Now I'm a mixture of Canul and O'Malley." He moved them both over to the sofa, and they got comfortable. "It's a long story."

She leaned in to him. "I've got time."

"It's ugly."

She heard a tremor in his voice. He'd only shown that level of emotion when she'd been hurt in Turkey. Shit, this was going to be bad.

"Handsome, I can handle ugly." She raised his arm, and then placed it around her shoulders. Of course, he was careful of her. She nestled in beside him, offering him comfort.

"We had it good," he began. "We were a tight unit, the three of us. Dad was former Navy, and he had a lot of friends, from his Navy days, and on the force. Their wives were Mom's friends. Me, I had the guys from school, but I also had friends from the neighborhood. We didn't live in the greatest section of town, but Dad liked it that way. He said that it was good that you policed where you lived. It gave you credibility. I always thought he was right."

Aiden paused. He was lost in thought.

"I had the best parents in the world, then there was Sam Chang, he was dad's partner. He and his wife NiNi were like a second set of parents." Aiden's thumb brushed idly against her collarbone.

"Dad and Sam were working on a big case. Hell, they were part of a task force, but it was a gang that was in our neighborhood. The Deuces. I even knew some of the guys. So did Dad. He was second in command on the case."

God, she didn't like where this was going.

"Derek, he was the head of the gang, he warned Dad off. Like Dad was going to listen. There had been so much violence in the neighborhood, it had to stop."

"How long ago was this?" Evie asked as she burrowed in closer to his side.

"Twenty-one years ago."

"You were fifteen?"

"Yep."

"So what happened?" she asked softly.

He didn't answer for a long while. She held her breath.

"There was an away game. Normally Mom and Dad would have come, but Dad was putting in overtime, and Mom didn't drive. When I got back to the school that night, Dad wasn't there to pick me up. I had Aaron's mom drop me off."

"When I went to unlock the door, it was already open. I thought maybe they heard me coming up the porch steps. I called out, but nobody answered." She felt him shudder. She didn't say anything, knowing he had to get it out.

Aiden started talking in a monotone voice, almost as if he were delivering a police report. Almost like his dad would have. "The living room was in shambles. Shit all knocked over; there had been a fight. Then there was a smear of blood leading down towards the bedrooms. Mom and Dad's door was closed. I opened it. Dad was duct taped to a kitchen chair. His eyes were taped open. There was a knife sticking out of his head."

"Mom was tied naked, spread eagle on the bed. I knew what had happened. They'd made Dad watch. She had a knife sticking out of her stomach." His voice broke for just a moment. "Blood was everywhere."

He swallowed, then continued in that flat voice. "I took a blanket and covered her and called Sam. I don't remember anything else that night. I woke up at Sam and NiNi's house."

Like Aiden, she didn't remember when they started, but Evie tears were streaming down her face. Aiden was holding her tight. It hurt, but she didn't care.

"It didn't end there, Eva."

"Tell me."

"The task force had a plan in place to take down Derek and most of his high level crew. They said that in a month after they had the head of the snake, they would take out the soldiers who had done that to my mom and dad. But I couldn't wait."

"What did you do?"

He looked down at her, his blue eyes ice cold. "I used my contacts to find the four guys who'd done it. I stalked them. I killed each and every one of them."

"You were only fifteen," she gasped.

"Didn't matter."

"It took me two weeks. It put a wrench in the task force's plans. Chicago PD was pissed, they were sure it was me, but they couldn't prove it. Meanwhile, Derek was gunning for me, which was fine, I was after him. But his reach was long and far. Sam reached out to Uncle Leonard and got me down to Veracruz."

Evie twisted around so she could look into his eyes. "You were only fifteen."

"It wouldn't have mattered if I'd been twelve, it still would have gone down the same way."

Looking into his arctic blue eyes, she believed him.

"You see it now, don't you? Well, it's more than that I'm just a killer."

She jerked as if she'd been hit. "You're not a killer!"

"Careful, Kitten. Don't hurt yourself." He put his hands on her waist and moved her so that she was cradled on his lap. "Make no mistake, I hunted those four men down, and I killed them in cold blood."

"If you hadn't, I would have," she muttered. "Is that why you broke things off with us, you thought I would care about that?"

"Well, you should. For God's sake, Eva, think about the type of man you'd be getting involved with."

"A good man. A decent man. A man I would always want at my side. The man who came and rescued me. You're a hero."

He barked out a laugh.

"I'm the furthest thing from a hero imaginable."

"Is that why you did the one-eighty in Tennessee?"

She watched as sadness engulfed his face. "No. Something happened three months ago."

"What."

"NiNi was killed."

She gasped. More tears fell. "Not Sam's wife. Oh Aiden, I'm so sorry."

"Derek had been paroled last year, so I was sure that the Deuces had started up on their promises of retribution."

"But that wasn't what happened?"

"No, Sam called right before I left for Turkey. It was a random act of violence. They caught the killer, he had nothing to do with Derek or the Deuces."

Evie tried to think through everything Aiden hadn't said.

"Are you saying that you were trying to protect me?"

"Eva, Sam was small potatoes compared to me. I was the big get. That meant anybody close to me had a huge target on their chest. Hell yes, I wanted to protect you," he said vehemently. "Plus there's the added fact that I'm just not the man you thought I was."

"Gah!" She struggled to get up, but he held her gently, stopping her from going anywhere. "Let me up!"

"Eva, you're going to hurt yourself."

"I wouldn't if you would just let me up. I refuse to be held by such a stupid man."

"Calm."

"Fuck your calm. Stop with the one word commands. I'm not a dog."

"Please, Eva, I'm begging you, you'll hurt yourself. And I really need to hold you."

Shit, he'd said the right thing. She calmed down and settled back on his lap.

He rubbed his cheek against hers. "Why am I stupid?" he asked in a whisper.

"Because even at fifteen you were a hero. You stood up for yourself. For your parents. You're everything I'm not. If anything, you should run from me."

"There isn't anything you could tell me about yourself that would make me think less of you. You shine. Telling you this has helped chase away the darkness."

"At least you fought," she said forlornly.

Chapter Fifteen

Aiden's gut clenched. He breathed in through his nose. Evie not fight? He couldn't imagine it.

"Tell me, Kitten," he coaxed.

"It was after Dad went to prison and Drake went into the Navy. Things were totally out of control. I had to quit school. Trenda had already graduated, thank God, but she and I were both working because Mom wasn't. We were trying to support the household."

"How old were you?" he asked quietly.

"Older than you were." Her tone was bitter.

"How old?" he coaxed.

"Sixteen." She sighed. She didn't say anything else; she seemed lost in thought.

"So what did you do?" he finally prompted.

"I started working as a maid. Trenda started waitressing at the truck stop outside of town. Maddie was fourteen, the twins were eleven, and Piper was six."

Aiden couldn't imagine that kind of responsibility heaped on such young shoulders. "Didn't anyone help out? Relatives?

Friends of the family? Neighbors?" He couldn't help the bite in his tone.

"Granny Laughton was already so old and frail that she couldn't help. The neighbors thought we were trash, except for the lady who ran the food bank. Thank God for her."

"There was nobody else?"

"Uncle Huey," her voice was so low he had to strain to hear her.

Aiden remembered the rotten piece of garbage. He had ended up in prison. He'd been in cahoots with Evie's dad, running drugs in Sevier County. Goddammit. He'd known. He'd known deep down that the fucker was evil as soon as Drake had told the story of him siccing the dog on Maddie.

"He did more than not help, didn't he?" Evie gave an imperceptible nod.

"What did he do?"

"Trenda and I just weren't paying attention. Maddie thought she could do something to help the family. She was just a baby but she was trying to help. She was only fourteen Aiden," Evie's whisper was filled with pain.

"What did that motherfucker do?"

"He had a dry cleaning business, and they did pick-up and delivery."

Aiden remembered it was a front for drugs.

"She did some deliveries," he surmised.

Evie nodded. "I swear to fucking God, he arranged for her to get caught, so he could hold it over her head. But he had that crooked sheriff, Delmar Arnold, pick her up. They took her to county jail for the afternoon. She should have called us, but Huey visited her, him being family and all." Evie's eyes were dry and bitter. She looked like she might shatter at any instant.

"Then what?"

"He said that he could pay off the cops, but it would cost more than she could ever make just with the drop-offs."

What the fuck would that monster make his fourteen-year-old niece do?

"I found her at home, she was sneaking through Trenda's underwear drawer. I demanded to know what she was doing, and that's when she broke down and told me everything. Including the fact that she was supposed to wear pretty lingerie for a modeling shoot at Uncle Huey's trailer."

Ice froze his veins. He could see the rage in her eyes. "I grabbed her arm and took her to Mom. I screamed at her; told her what was going on. Do you know what she said? She said Maddie made her bed and she had to lie in it."

Aiden closed his eyes. It was unimaginable to him that a mother could have said something like that.

Evie must have seen his disgust.

"Exactly. You can't even wrap your head around it! Do you know what I did?"

He shook his head.

"I slapped her."

"Good." And he meant it. She deserved a hell of a lot more than a slap in his opinion.

"Really? I mean she was my mother. Is. Is my mother." Evie was breathing hard.

"For God's sake, she conspired to kill Piper and Drake. She stopped being your mother the moment she hung Maddie out to dry. You should have punched her."

Evie gave a dry half laugh. "Yeah, I should have, especially considering."

He hugged her closer. "Considering what?"

"Aiden, you're a miracle."

Huh? That was confusing. "What are you talking about, Kitten?"

"I don't feel dirty anymore."

Fuck. Jesus. He wasn't going to like this. "You're not dirty. I told you, you shine. You're pure."

She gave a hollow laugh. "Let's not get carried away. Let me finish this."

"Spit it out."

He knew though. She switched places with Maddie. Of course, she had.

"I drove over to Huey's dirty little trailer. My aunt wasn't there, or my cousin Harmon. Just Huey and the sheriff. God, I made such a mistake. The sheriff was holding a camera, and laughing his ass off. Said he got the feisty one."

"I told them that the charges were bullshit, and I'd call the FBI."

"The sheriff told me nobody would ever believe some white trash whore whose dad was in prison over the sheriff."

"I was so stupid, I should have just run away, gotten into my car and run. Instead, I tried to make a deal with them not to press charges against Maddie. So fucking stupid." He barely stopped her before she slapped her forehead.

"Hey, none of that. You were sixteen. You'd quit school to take care of your family. You were in way over your head. Your mother and your uncle had betrayed you."

"Huey told me I could take Maddie's place, and they'd call it a day."

"I spit at him." She stared off into space for a long moment. "It was the wrong thing to do."

"The sheriff grabbed me from behind, and Huey took off his belt. They stripped me. Huey about lost his mind. But the sheriff stopped him. Said it was bad for the pictures. The sheriff knelt in front of me. Actually knelt."

She looked up at him, lost in memories. He could see that the moment had amazed her.

"Then what, Baby?"

"He told me what to do. His whispers were sly like a snake. His hands shook when he posed me."

"He touched you." It wasn't a question, it was a statement.

"Not like that, just to pose me."

"He touched you." Aiden saw it all in his head, a sixteen-year-old girl, red welts all over her body, being posed by a fat man in a uniform.

"But I let them Aiden. I just let the sheriff touch me. Move me. Huey took the pictures. It was like I was in a trance. I only woke up when I heard cousin Harmon's truck pull up. It was the same for Huey and the sheriff. They threw my clothes at me and told me to get dressed."

Aiden forced himself to relax when all he wanted to do was clutch her close. But she was still healing, and he didn't want to harm her.

"Huey grabbed me as Harmon came in. Said it wasn't over. Said I had to come back the next day. That's when I grew a brain."

"What do you mean?"

"I told him I was going to call Drake. It was like I said a magic word. Ever since Drake testified against Dad and put him away, Huey had been scared as shit of him. I should have used his name from the get-go. Fuck, I should have called Drake, except he was told never to come back to town. But still, he would have for Maddie. I was so fucking stupid.

Finally, he could touch her and not crush her. Softly. He kissed the top of her head. "You weren't stupid. You were young."

"I still surf porn sites looking for my pictures."

"You've got to stop that, Eva. It's behind you."

"You were brave. I just took it."

"Are you kidding? You protected your sister. You're fierce."

"Stupid."

He was getting frustrated. "Kitten, Piper's eighteen, if she'd gone to that trailer, would you call her stupid?"

"She's been sheltered. It's not the same thing at all. It's like comparing apples and oranges. I was dumber than a stump." Her Southern accent was thick.

Okay, now he *was* pissed. "If you put down my woman one more time, you won't like the consequences. She shines like sunshine, and is pure as snow."

She opened her mouth to disagree, then closed it, then opened it again. "Your woman?"

"Well, yes, why else would I be baring my soul? I told you. I was a deliberate ass to you in Tennessee so you'd hate me because I thought you'd end up being a target. Now I know it wasn't true, and you can handle who I really am. Damn right, I'm claiming you."

"You're claiming me?"

"Have you turned into a parrot?"

Evie's eyes were wide as she stared up at him.

"I think you have this all wrong, Handsome. If you're under the mistaken impression I'm still pure as snow, then I'm claiming you."

"Thank, Jesus." His head dipped, and he took her mouth, hard. He needed to possess this woman, make sure she knew that she belonged to him. She opened her mouth and welcomed his advance.

Deep. Wet. Hot.

Her kiss, her touch, her taste, sustained him.

Made him whole.

She whimpered. Dammit. What was he thinking? Not only was she not healed, she had just told him about a traumatic event. He was a bastard. He lifted his head.

She grabbed his hair and tried to pull him back down.

"Aiden, why did you stop?"

"I'm not stopping, I'm slowing down." He kissed her lightly, sweetly, lingering, on the lips.

"Well don't. Speed up." He smiled and looked into her fevered brown eyes. He brushed back the hair from her temple.

"Now that I know you're mine, we have all the time in the world."

Her hands stopped threading through the hair at the back of his neck. "So you're saying now isn't the right time?"

"I'm saying that you're still healing."

It was as if a wall shut down on her features. One second she was Evie, all radiant and wanton, then she was stiff as a board. Lifeless.

"Eva, where did you go?"

"Let me up," she said woodenly.

Aiden thought through the last minute and realized his mistake. If he could, he'd have kicked his own ass. "Kitten, please, listen. I want you. This isn't about your past."

"Let me up," she repeated.

"I thought after all of your revelations, and the fact that you're still healing, that I'd be a bastard to take advantage of you at this moment. Just one more day. Can we wait until tomorrow night?"

"Aiden, let me up. I'm begging you." Finally some emotion. But the wrong kind. It was desperation.

To hell with this. He heaved up, lifting them both off the couch in one motion.

"Aiden. No."

He aimed for his bedroom, ignoring her protest. He'd fucked up enough.

Chapter Sixteen

Evie clung to Aiden's arms. She knew where they were headed. Part of her wanted to protest, part of her wanted to bolt. Instead, she melted into his hold. This was where she wanted to be, even if he was only being nice.

He opened the door at the end of the hall. She'd never been in his room. It was big and bold, just like the man. He put her put her down in such a way that she slid against his big body, and she realized in no uncertain terms he was just as enthusiastic about this as she was. He shut the door and locked it. Her breath hitched for just a moment. He saw it.

"Do you want me to unlock the door?"

For a second she had a vision of Bella wandering the hall. "Oh no, locked is good."

"Come here." His voice was hoarse.

She took the three steps to meet him. She looked up and up and up until her eyes met his glittering blue ones. "Are you absolutely sure? I don't want to hurt you physically or emotionally."

She placed her hands on his chest. It was time to be brave. "I love you, Aiden, you could never frighten me."

He shuddered at her words. "You mean the world to me." He took her right hand and kissed her palm. "I love you too, Kitten."

Her knees went weak. He caught her up in his arms and carried her to his bed.

He came down with her and gathered her close.

Why was he watching her so carefully? Would he please stop? But then she realized she was doing the same thing. This was important. This meant something. This meant everything.

"Aiden?"

"Yes, Eva?"

"This is real? This is really going to happen? I wanted it back in Tennessee. I wanted it so bad." She thought back to those kisses, where she thought things were leading…

"Yes, Baby, this is real. It was real in Tennessee, I swear. I should never have left you." She melted at his words. He brushed his fingertips across her collarbone. She shuddered. He traced a path to her left shoulder, and pushed the delicate cotton out of the way. He bent and kissed her there, even though the bruises had faded.

"You've been driving me crazy. You haven't been wearing a bra."

"The straps would have hurt my shoulder. Anyway, I don't need one." She paused. "You really noticed?"

Aiden slowly peeled away her gauzy blouse, revealing her tank top. "Oh, I noticed."

She smiled. Then her smile turned hazy as he grazed the back of his hand over the tip of her breast. "God, do that again."

He turned his hand over, and cupped her, his thumb brushed across her nipple. She pushed against him, as she started to yank up her tank.

"Let me," he said.

"You take off your shirt," she demanded.

He chuckled and levered off her.

She watched in rapt fascination as he did that man thing where he reached behind his shoulders with one hand and pulled the t-shirt over the back of his head.

Oh God.

Oh God.

Oh God.

He looked better than she'd imagined. All that luscious muscle with golden chest hair sprinkled over it, arrowing downward over a powerfully ripped abdomen. She wasn't even aware of a conscious decision to touch, but she saw her hands splayed against his chest, and felt all that warmth and power against her palms and she trembled with want.

"Eva, are you listening?"

"Are you talking?"

He laughed.

"This is going to be fun. We are on the same page. I need you to lift your arms."

"Oh. Oh yeah." She flushed.

"Hey, nothing to be embarrassed about. I feel the same way. I can't wait to get this shirt off you."

She didn't think it would be the same at all. She knew what was under the tank top. And she wasn't a goddess, whereas he was a Greek god. But she wasn't a coward. She lifted her arms, and he pulled off the tank. Damn, she shouldn't have done that.

"Dammit. Would you have a care?" he admonished.

Then he sucked in a breath. "My God, you're beautiful."

Well, what else would he say?

"Lie back."

She must have taken too long because he guided her back down onto the bed.

"So delicate, so feminine, I knew you would be the most beautiful woman I would ever have in my bed." His eyes flickered between her face to her breasts and back up again.

"I have to taste you."

She would die if he didn't.

The first touch of his lips shot through her like a bolt of electricity. So gentle, but so stunning, she could do nothing but hope to somehow to survive the most joyous moment of her life.

At some point, Aiden must have looked up. "Baby!"

"Don't stop."

"You're crying."

"It's so much. So good. You like me. You love me. It's everything."

His thumbs swept up the tears on her cheeks. "Don't cry."

"These are happy tears."

"You're breaking my heart."

She wrapped her arms around his neck. "I'm so happy. You make me feel cherished."

"That's exactly how I want you to feel."

She placed a kiss over his heart. "Killing me," he said.

"Make love to me."

He gave her a long look, then kissed her. Deep and wet.

His fingers stroked down her stomach and touched the puckered skin where her stitches had been removed. He stilled. She pulled her head away. "Don't think about it. Now is now."

So much feeling was in his eyes. "I almost lost you."

"You have me."

He moved downwards, trailing kisses until he could caress her abused flesh with his lips. It was as if he were trying to heal her.

"Are you sure you're ready for this?" he asked again.

"So sure," she breathed. When his hand worked down the elastic band of her linen pants, she sighed with contentment. He stood beside the bed and divested himself of his jeans and briefs. She stared at him. Everything about this man called to her. She reached out to grasp his cock.

"No, if you do that I won't be able to last." He grimaced.

"Show some willpower," she said as her small hand glided over him. He chuckled, then grabbed her hand and kissed it, then knelt on the bed. He had her panties off in an instant. When he stroked a finger between her thighs, she bucked against his touch.

"You're so ready for me."

"God, yes. Please. Now."

He leaned over and opened his nightstand drawer and pulled out a condom. He tossed it on the pillow beside her head. She reached up to open it.

"In a minute or ten." He settled between her thighs, looking at her delicate flesh.

He wouldn't.

It would be too much.

His fingers touched her.

His lips kissed her.

His tongue caressed her.

She shot off into space.

"Eva?"

She looked up, and his eyes were next to hers; he was grinning. Well, he had every right. He was lying on his back and his cock was sheathed. He pulled her on top of him and gave her a long, slow, sweet kiss. The man could kiss. Soon, she was straddling him. She knew he was worried about her injuries, but she didn't know if she could do it this way. He saw her apprehension.

"It's just like riding a bike."

She snorted.

He guided her movements, and ever so slowly she took him into her body. He supported her with one big hand on her bottom, and another on her tummy, his thumb brushed along the top of her sex. As the rhythm started his thumb moved and swirled in time with his thrusts. Up and down. She lost herself in a maelstrom of passion as she looked into the bluest eyes she'd ever seen.

"I love you."

The words were said at the same time as they catapulted into bliss.

* * *

Aiden woke up, sure that he'd heard something. He looked at Evie sleeping soundly in his arms. Now he was having dreams. He'd definitely heard a woman's familiar voice. Maybe it was Trenda. He brushed a kiss on top of Evie's hair, then slipped from the bed.

He unlocked the bedroom door and padded down the hall. Trenda and Bella's door was firmly closed, the other bedroom doors were open. He went around the house and checked the doors and windows to make sure everything was secure and the alarm was set. Not that he hadn't done it already, but he felt like rechecking everything.

He got two bottles of water out of the refrigerator and went back to his room. Evie was sitting up in bed.

"Bad dream?" he asked.

"The worst. You left the bed without waking me up," she said as she waggled her fingers for a bottle. He smiled as he handed it to her.

"I thought I heard Trenda, and I woke up."

"Was she up?"

"No, I thought I heard her say, 'It's not finished. He's coming.' It was the weirdest thing. At first, I thought you said it, but you were asleep."

"That is weird."

"I swear I've heard the voice before."

"Maybe you were dreaming?"

"Maybe," he said dubiously.

"Get back under the covers. I have an idea of what can take your mind off things."

Aiden peeled back the duvet and revealed her gleaming body. She was right, all thoughts of his dream fled his mind.

* * *

Bella was all smiles the next morning, her temper tantrum completely forgotten. She was in the kitchen sitting on the counter watching her mother pour batter into the skillet.

"Pretty!" she clapped.

"Everybody gets special pancakes today. You get a smiley face," Trenda told her daughter. She picked her up and put her on the floor. "Go help Aunt Evie set the table."

Aiden had already gone for a run and was now in his office taking a phone call. He'd said he'd be out in time for breakfast, so Evie set four places for breakfast.

"I got a call from Maddie," Trenda said from the kitchen.

"Oh yeah? What did she have to say?"

"She heard the news about Jim and Blake putting the hotel on the market. She wanted to know if I knew anything about it."

"What did you say?" Evie asked as she pulled the orange juice out of the refrigerator.

"What could I say? I don't know anything. I figured that your knight in shining armor probably had a talk with Jim and said get the hell out of town, but I can't be sure of that, now can I?"

Evie listened to the sizzle of bacon.

"I helped," Bella said as she folded the napkins and set them beside each of the plates.

"Yes you did, Sweetie." Evie looked at Trenda who was putting pancakes on two separate platters. "Yes, Aiden had a talk with them. I didn't agree, and I think he went too far. He thought having them there would be a reminder to me."

"Baby Girl, it's also a punishment to them for being… well…fill in the blanks with really nasty swear words. Jim needed to pay for what was done to you."

Evie opened her mouth to protest, and Trenda held up the tongs she was holding. "I don't want to hear it. He got off easy. I didn't hear about any broken bones. I didn't hear about him dying. I just heard he's selling his property and moving. Don't expect me to feel bad for him."

"What about Blake?"

"He's chosen that bed to lie in." Trenda flipped a pancake and took the bacon off the burner.

"I like the way you think, Trenda," Aiden said as he came into the room.

"Shut up both of you. Blake was dragged to Turkey just like I was."

"Do I smell bacon?" Aiden asked.

"You're really going to say that and now transition to bacon?"

"You asked me to shut up," he said reasonably.

Fuck, he was right.

"Sit down, Aiden. I don't want her appetite ruined. You I don't worry about."

"Mama made pretty pancakes. I helped setted the table." Bella beamed up at the tall man. He set her down in the booster seat that he had somehow arranged to have at his house. It was one more thing that made her heart melt.

Evie sat down next to Aiden, and Trenda placed a platter of heart shaped pancakes between them. Aiden burst out laughing.

"Seemed like the right occasion." Trenda smiled. Damn, nothing got by her sister.

"What, no red food coloring?" Evie asked.

"Nope, couldn't find any. However, I did make some raspberry syrup."

"I've died and gone to heaven," Aiden said. He placed two pancakes on Evie's plate then stacked three times as many on his.

"I got a smiley face!" Bella said pointing to her plate.

Soon they were all eating breakfast.

She was going to miss them when they left. She looked up and saw that Trenda was smiling at her sadly. Damn, the woman was reading her mind again.

Chapter Seventeen

Evie hated to see her sister and niece leave. Drake had picked her up from Aiden's house, and Evie had gone with them to the airport. He might tower over his sisters, but there was no denying the family resemblance, and people stared as they hugged at security.

"I'll think about everything you've said," Trenda promised her brother. Then she and Drake looked at Evie.

"Don't look at me, I'm undecided, too." It was too damn much pressure. She didn't have a home to go back to in Tennessee. As much as she loved her older sister, she didn't want to live with her. The hotel was no longer an option. But she didn't have a job in San Diego, so she didn't know what she was going to do.

"Oh, Baby Girl, I'm not trying to put pressure on you. You're still recovering. But you will always have a home with me."

"And me," Drake said quickly.

And Aiden. He'd said so on numerous occasions, but she didn't want to just move in because he thought she needed a place to stay. Moving from Tennessee to San Diego was a huge step. But she'd do it if he really meant it as the next step in their relationship. She loved him. She wanted to build a life with him, but was it too soon?

"Evie?" She looked at Trenda.

"Are you okay?"

"I'm just going to miss you."

"That's not it, but I'll let it slide. You call me tonight." God, nothing got by the woman. She plucked Bella out of her sister's arms and blew a raspberry on the little girl's neck.

"I'm gonna ride on a plane!"

"Yes, you are!"

"I'm going to see the Aunt Owies!" Everybody laughed at her name for Chloe and Zoe.

"Come on, Pumpkin, we've gotta go." Trenda tried to take her daughter back, but Drake took her from Evie's arms and threw her up in the air. People around the area smiled at Bella's delighted laughter.

"Who's your favorite uncle?" he asked.

"Uncle Dwake!"

"God, I'm going to hate it when you learn how to say my name right," he lamented.

"Give me my daughter," Trenda said sternly.

Drake sighed.

He cuddled Bella close one last time, then gave her over to Trenda and cupped the little girl's head for one last kiss. "I love you, Bella. Take care of your mama for me." Bella turned to her mother and patted her cheek.

"I take care of her. I love her too."

Evie felt tears forming. Bella was definitely an Avery, but the idea of a little towheaded girl or boy was precious. She blinked fast. Damn, she'd be happy when she didn't need the pain pills. They were making her too emotional.

Drake dropped a careful arm around her shoulders as they headed back toward the parking lot.

"So what's the scoop with you and Aiden?"

"There's no scoop."

"Bullshit," he said mildly as he helped her into the passenger seat. "That man has you marked as his territory, and what's more, you're in love." With that, he shut the door and walked around to the driver's side. It still didn't give her enough time to come up with an appropriate response.

"Got nothing?" he asked as he started the car.

"He doesn't look at me like I'm his territory."

"If he were a Southern boy, I'd say he was going to piss around you."

She snorted. "Are you saying you were going to piss around Karen?"

"I was going to do whatever it took to make sure that she was tagged and treed. She's mine, and nobody ought to be confused about that fact." He pulled onto the freeway with a satisfied smile on his face. It was good to see Drake so happy.

Was Aiden as happy with her?

Drake looked at her sideways. "Are you getting confused, Evalyn Lavender? That boy is gone over you. I don't know what happened in Tennessee, but he's got his head out of his ass now."

She laughed. Drake had a way with words.

"If I stayed here in San Diego, what would I do? Jim and Blake let me be a jack of all trades. I did everything from cleaning and booking rooms, to handling events. But I don't think any fancy hotels out here would get past the fact that I was a maid."

"Go to school."

"I'm too old to go to school. It was painful enough to get my GED."

Drake was silent until he pulled off the freeway. "Why was it hard for you to get your GED? I remember you tutoring Maggie and the twins. Wasn't math one of your best subjects?"

"You remember that?"

"Sure. I had to really work at math, so I was impressed. Why was the GED hard?"

Evie thought back to the time when she was working over forty hours a week cleaning the LeeHy Motel, going home and making sure that Mom had actually gotten the twins and Piper fed. In between that, she scrambled to work on getting her GED. Those two years passed in a blur.

"I wasn't as strong in the other subjects," she lied. She didn't want Drake to know how bad it had been.

"So get a degree in math. Shit, Evie, companies are crying for people with degrees in math and science. You'll kick ass."

"College costs a lot."

"Let's not forget the money that's going to be coming to Piper. Granny Laughton's land is going to sell next month. Those companies really drove the price up when they saw the natural gas surveys."

"That's Piper's money."

"Shut it. Piper's already talked to us about parsing it out. I'm not taking any of it, but you sure as hell are."

That pissed her off. They pulled into the parking spot for the apartment. As soon as Drake put the truck into park, Evie grabbed his arm. "Let me tell you something, you dumbass. I'm not taking a fucking dime if you aren't."

"Karen and I make great livings."

"You have a baby on the way, and you need a house, and eventually you're going to need to pay for Caroline's college education. If you expect me to take some of the money that Piper's giving out, then you're taking some of it, too."

"Granny would want it to go to you girls."

"For God's sake, she would want it to go to *all* of her grandchildren, not just the ones with vaginas!"

Drake let out a huge laugh. "Did you just say vaginas?"

"Yeah, haven't you heard of those before?"

"Nope, never have."

Evie started to giggle. Then she started to laugh.

"Oh, shit, you're a pistol."

"So it's agreed, you're taking some of the money?"

"Are you going to shack up with Aiden and go to school?" he asked.

"I'm going to go to school. I don't know where I'm going to live yet. All the girls are in Tennessee."

"Trenda's thinking about moving out here," Drake said quietly. He motioned his head, and she opened her door. "Wait for me."

"I can get out on my own."

"You're tiny, the truck's big, and you're still healing."

"Gah! Save me from bossy men."

He came around and helped her out of the truck. How in the hell had he turned into such a gentlemen coming from Wanda and Norville? It was a freaking miracle. Actually, it was amazing that all of the kids had turned out as well as they had, she thought.

"Piper can't wait to tell you about her first week of classes."

"She already has. She's been on the phone almost every day."

"Yeah, but now you get facial expressions and hand gestures. Seriously, Evie, our Tinkerbell is so damned excited, I'm over the moon. After the shit that went down with Mom and Dad, I never guessed she could be this happy so soon."

"You and Karen have a lot to do with this."

"Well, come on in, and be prepared to be overwhelmed."

"Gotchya."

* * *

"Yeah, it happened before the sale went through. Chased away the buyers," Dex said.

Aiden stopped using all of his focus on Evie's body, which was displayed beautifully in a bikini on the patio.

"What did you say?"

"I said that Jim still hasn't sold the hotel."

"Yeah, but why? What happened exactly?"

"The office was ransacked. Scared the new buyers. They'd been told that the place had a state-of-the art security system."

"State-of-the-art was pushing it, but for Jasper Creek, it was pretty damn good. If nothing else, it should have been enough of a deterrent to have someone go looking for easier pickings. Why would they ransack the place? There's nothing of value there, it's in the middle of nowhere. Was the safe found?"

"Not only was the floor safe found, they actually got it open."

Aiden's eyebrows raised. That was no easy feat. It had taken him a half-hour the first time when he had gone to check on Evie's whereabouts. His uncle would have been so disappointed at his poor performance.

"So this was a professional hit," Aiden said.

"Well, whoever it was, they were determined. They used C-4 to get it open."

"Holy hell. They *were* serious. And all this happened after they had cleared out?"

"Yep. The perps would have come away empty."

This was giving Aiden a bad feeling. "Dex, I want you to dig into their past. I want you to go over them with a fine-tooth comb. We've been assuming that Jim was just a patsy, but maybe it was something more."

"You've got a bad feeling?"

"Call my uncle if you need to, just make sure you have checked every angle possible."

"I'm on it."

"Also-" Aiden stopped himself.

"What?"

He continued to look at all of the beauty and purity that was Evie. "Never mind. I've got this covered."

"Well if you need anything, you know where to find me."

"Always. And thanks, Dex."

He disconnected the call, then roamed through his contacts until he found the name, Rylie Jones. She was soon to be married to Darius Stanton. He'd only met her once, but he enjoyed the hell out of her. But he was calling because of all of the stories he had heard about her. He had her number because he collected numbers and contacts. A man was foolish not to.

He dialed, and instead of her answering 'Hello,' she knew it was him.

"Aiden, imagine my surprise to be getting a call from our Drake's soon to be brother-in-law."

"And here I was going to say something nice to you, Rylie." Aiden grinned. This was the reason he liked her. He'd enjoyed sparring with the little spitfire. When he'd been missing Evie, it was a little like being around her.

"You weren't going to say anything nice to me," she disagreed. "If you had bothered to track down my number, you were going to ask a favor. I'm warning you now, I believe in quid pro quo."

"Who are you talking to?" he heard Dare Stanton's voice in the background.

"Adam Levine needs a favor, I'm asking him to write a song for me. Let me negotiate," she fired back.

Aiden heard Darius laugh. Rylie had that power over people. "Okay, O'Malley, what do you need? Know it's going to cost you, I've pulled your financials."

"For this, you can name your price. The deal is, it remains between the two of us."

There was a long pause. "I don't keep secrets from Dare," she finally said.

"Hear me out."

"This better be good. Otherwise, I'm going to be mad that you asked me to betray my man's trust."

Aiden gathered his thoughts as he looked at Evie. All that mattered was protecting her; making sure that she knew those images were gone, and she never had to go trolling the internet again.

He told Rylie the ugly story of two men forcing a sixteen-year-old Evie to take nude pictures after they had whipped her.

"Those motherfuckers! I'll kill them."

"Down girl, they're in prison."

"Which one? Which cell block? These things matter." Shit, Aiden hadn't considered that.

"Never mind, I'll find out."

"I wasn't calling you so you could torture Huey and the sheriff," Aiden reminded her.

"That's just an extra service. I know why you're calling. This is going to take a while. I'm going to have to do some digging to find out all the pictures. How many years ago was this when it happened? I need a timeframe."

"Eight years ago. Like I said, she was sixteen."

"That sick fuck and he was trying to get her fourteen-year-old sister too? Oh yeah, I'm going after them. If they're not in the worst cell block, then I'm arranging a transfer."

Aiden didn't think Dex could even get that done. Rylie was crazy scary. "Do you think you can track down the pictures?"

There was a long pause. "Yeah, I think I can. The problem is getting them off the internet. I might get them taken down for a while, but people will have downloaded them, and after I've gotten them off a site, then somebody with a private collection might re-upload them. It's a never-ending battle. But with facial recognition software, we can keep at it."

"Fuck!" He looked at Evie, and his heart broke.

"You have options," she said quietly. "Most people don't know everything I do about how the internet operates."

"What do you mean?"

"When the time comes, tell her that everything has been taken down. Leave it at that. I'll have web-crawlers set up to find and take them down as soon as the pictures reappear. But she doesn't have to know that it will always be a problem."

He pressed his fingers against the bridge of his nose. It helped relieve some of the pressure. "You're going to tell Dare, aren't you?"

"Drake doesn't know, does he?" Rylie asked cautiously. "Dare won't break the trust of our relationship, I promise you."

"Thank you." And he meant it. "The same reason you're going to tell Dare is why I'm going to tell Evie the truth. I don't want to keep anything from her, that's not how I want us to be. We'll celebrate the day they're down, and then I'll tell her all you're doing to keep them from showing back up."

"I'm so happy for you. Not for nothing, I think you're doing the right thing." He could hear the warmth in her voice.

"I'm going to get to work on this today."

"What's your hourly rate?"

"Don't insult me."

"Seriously, this is a huge assignment. I'm going to pay. If you don't charge me, then I'll go somewhere else."

She blew out a breath. "There's a children's home in Oklahoma that needs donations."

"Done. Just tell me where to send the check."

Chapter Eighteen

She couldn't catch her breath. His hand smoothed up her hip. She loved how he felt, his hands were so big, slightly rough, warm, but more than anything, his touch was loving.

"Eyes on me." She lifted her heavy lids. He always expected her to keep her eyes open. It was so difficult when sensation after sensation pummeled her system. But then she'd see his beautiful face and wonder why she ever closed them.

"There's my girl."

She smiled. He cupped her breast at the same time his leg slid between hers. He was still careful with her. It drove her crazy. She needed his power. Tonight, she was changing things. She curled her thigh around his hip.

He pressed her leg against the mattress. "Uh-uh. We're taking this easy."

She trapped his other hand against her breast and this time curled her right thigh around his hips.

"Kitten, I'm serious," he groaned as her core ground against his cock.

"I want you on top tonight."

"You're still not healed."

"It's been five weeks, I need to feel you holding me, surrounding me, enveloping me." She felt him shudder. She was going to win.

He bent his head and lapped at her nipple and sizzles streaked up her spine. His other hand cupped her ass, bringing her even closer. More pleasure arced through her. His body rasped against hers, every place they connected was another form of bliss. How could someone so raw and masculine be so beautiful and gentle? The dichotomy made her breathless.

"Are you sure?" he asked as he nuzzled her cheek.

"Yes."

His eyes searched hers, and he must have been assured because a huge grin split his face. Their lips met, and it was another glorious wet, wild, mind-blowing kiss. Soon he was filling her, and it was just as she'd hoped. She knew he was still careful, but it felt wonderful to be enclosed in his arms with his heat filling her.

Her nails dug into his muscled back.

"Harder Eva," he groaned. She dug in harder and scraped. She saw his eyes glint with pleasure. He thrust deeper, and she moaned.

He moved his hand to touch her. "No, I don't need it," she panted. She was almost there. She'd never been so turned on. She arched up. He angled down. He hit the right spot, and she went up in flames.

"Aiden!" she cried out, never wanting the moment to end.

* * *

"This time, will you listen when I ask you to live with me?"

Looking up at him, she shook her head. "Are you seriously trying to use your body to sway me?"

"Only if it works. Now if I need to try again, I'm willing to go for seconds."

She gave a small laugh.

"Eva, can you tell me what's stopping you?"

"Would you be asking me to live with you if I wasn't basically homeless?" She held her breath.

He brushed back a dark curl. "What part of 'you chase away the darkness' did you not understand?"

"But you've been holding *me* during *my* nightmares. You haven't had any nightmares," she protested.

"I buried them too deep. But they were there. I haven't talked about my mom and dad in over twenty years. Did you know that since I told you that story I've thought about some of our good times together? You did that. You're helping me heal."

Tears came fast. She couldn't stop them. The idea of him not having those good memories hurt her heart.

"Hey, don't cry. This is a good thing."

"I know."

"So, now you understand why I want you with me. This isn't pity, this is pure unadulterated selfishness. I love you, Eva, you make me happy. Please stay with me."

"I want to go to school. I won't know how much I can contribute until Granny's land sells," she warned him.

"For God's sake, I'm loaded. I'll pay for your school."

She reared back. "You'll do no such thing. I just want to warn you I don't know how much I can contribute to the household."

He rolled her over on the bed, and she found herself looking up into dark, flashing eyes. "You will not pay anything towards my house, except raspberry syrup. I want raspberry syrup. That, you're allowed to pay for. Are we clear?"

"So I guess I'm moving in."

"Thank the Lord, I finally got my way."

She dug her fingers into his ribs.

He yelped. "No fair."

"Just don't think sex got you your way. It was the pretty words."

His eyes softened. "They weren't just pretty words, they were the truth."

She kissed the middle of his chest, over his heart. "I love you, Aiden Carlos O'Malley. You chase away my darkness, too."

* * *

In the six weeks, since they'd returned from Turkey, they'd developed a routine. Aiden had been back in rotation for three weeks, and now he just asked for three days off to go to Tennessee with Evie. Blake and Jim had packed up all of her belongings and put them in a heated storage unit. Now she wanted to go through them and determine what would stay and what would go.

She'd explained that there was plenty of stuff that she would like to give to Maddie, Chloe, and Zoe. Maddie was meeting them at the storage locker, and then they were going out to dinner. She was the one sister that he hadn't met. Evie had been apprehensive about it.

"She's special. She's super smart. You know she's in a Master's program."

"Hey. What's this about? You think I'm going to hold something against her that she did when she was fourteen?"

Evie ducked her head, then she looked up. "Then there's the thing with that asshole boyfriend."

"I hold *you* responsible for that. If you ever try going after someone with a bat and don't call me for help, you're going over my knee. Are we clear?"

"Now you sound like my brother, and that's *not* a compliment."

"Eva, I love all of your sisters, Maddie isn't going to be the exception," he assured her. He smiled at her look of relief.

That had been two days ago in San Diego. Since that conversation, she had been burning up the telephone lines with Maddie, Chloe, and Zoe. She knew they were only going to be in Tennessee for two days and she planned to make the most of it.

Evie was practically vibrating with excitement. If she hadn't convinced him last night in bed, he'd be convinced today that she was completely healed.

"There's her car. Park there. She must be in the office." Evie pointed to a little white Toyota.

He parked the car, and as they were getting out, he saw Maddie Avery walking toward them wearing white shorts and a red top. "Hell, Evie, you *are* the shortest, aren't you?"

"Maddie!" she squealed.

The sisters ran to one another and hugged for a long moment. Then the younger girl burst into tears. Aiden wasn't surprised, Trenda had had a similar reaction when she'd first seen Evie. All of the women were emotional about Evie's kidnapping.

He could hear Evie soothing her sister. Maddie might be taller, but it was abundantly clear who was the 'big' sister.

"Come on, Honey, it's all right. Let's get out of the sun. We'll do the sorting later. We need to go get some iced tea. How does that sound?"

Soon they were in the rental car, and Evie pointed them toward a small building that said Polly's Restaurant. It was well known to both women. "It has the best pie in the world. You'll love it, Aiden."

"It can't be better than Trenda's pie," he said. It couldn't. That woman could bake.

"Wait and see," was all Evie would say.

Aiden split his concentration on the road and the rearview mirror, studying Maddie. She was studying him just as fiercely. It turned out that Evie had a protector. He was impressed.

Evie pointed to a tidy building. The parking lot was bursting at the seams. That was always a good sign. It reminded him of the café where Mason's wife worked.

"There's a spot," Evie said and pointed to an empty parking spot. He took it. He was hungry, but he resigned himself to a long wait since there were people sitting outside on the two benches.

"Why don't you go get us a table. You've been away for a while, and Polly will be ecstatic to see you."

Evie grinned and nodded. Aiden opened the door for her, and she went inside. Maddie didn't waste any time.

"So Evie's going to move in with you? Are you going to break her heart again?"

Aiden opened his mouth to say 'No,' when he took a moment to really look at Maddie. Her hands were open by her side, but they were trembling ever so slightly. When he looked into her eyes, he saw that behind the bravado, she was a little scared confronting him. But she was doing it anyway. Aiden admired that.

"Maddie, I promise you, I'm not going to hurt Evie ever again. I would cut off an arm before I would do anything to make her cry."

She swallowed. "Then why did you?"

"That's between me and her. But please know, I thought I was protecting her."

Maddie gripped the end of her ponytail and twirled it. "Evie's special. She would go to the mat for you, and it would be-" Her voice broke, and she looked down.

Aiden looked over and saw Evie still talking to the woman at the hostess stand. He guided Maddie to one of the benches that had just opened up and sat down with her.

"What, Honey?"

"She's so used to taking care of everyone else, it would just be nice if someone was finally watching her back. You know?"

"Consider me her protector."

"I thought I could trust Jim and Blake, and look what they did." She sounded so forlorn. The woman was right. Evie had been let down by so many men in her life, including him.

"Please be for real," she whispered.

"Maddie, she's my life."

She stopped fiddling with her hair and looked at him. Really looked at him, then nodded.

Out of the corner of his eye, he saw Evie heading toward the door. "Wait here." He got up and opened the door for her. "What's the wait time?" he asked.

"What wait time? Our table is ready. We're practically family." Maddie was already standing at his elbow.

"Well okay then, good food with two beautiful women, what more could a man ask for?"

* * *

They got a call at the restaurant that the twins were five miles out of town, so they headed back to the storage facility. When they got to their unit, they were waiting for them.

"What is this?" Evie demanded, looking at the dilapidated Ford 350 the twins had parked in front of the storage unit.

"It's Clive's. He let us borrow it," Zoe said.

Chloe laughed. "Let is a relative term. Zoe finally gave in and promised to go out with him if he would let us borrow it for the weekend."

"Why in the hell did you want to borrow this piece of shit?" Evie demanded looking at the red truck outfitted with a gun rack, stripper mud flaps, and silver nut sack hanging from the trailer hitch.

"We figured there would be some furniture we could have. We moved into a place off campus. I've been saving for some furniture, so I'm not sure how much we're going to take of yours. You know our tastes don't always match, Evie," Chloe explained cautiously.

Maddie let out a choked sound.

"Speak for yourself, I've always wanted those purple chairs. You'll never be able to find some of the stuff she has at any stinking furniture store," Zoe protested.

Aiden had forgotten about the purple chairs. Now that he thought about it, he was kind of glad she didn't want to take any of her furniture or fixtures to California.

"I saw that." Evie smacked her hand against his abdomen.

"What?"

"You just had a vision of my purple chairs in your living room, and you winced."

"I did not wince."

"He so didn't," Chloe agreed. "But he should have. Trenda showed us pictures of his house. It's the bomb. Seriously, you are not allowed to do any decorating. You and Zoe are never allowed near a furniture store."

"What are you talking about?" Zoe demanded of her twin.

"You're practically color blind. You chose turquoise, lemon, orange, and red to decorate the kitchen."

"Yeah, it rocks," Zoe said as Aiden opened up the large door of the storage unit.

"Score!" Zoe unhitched the back of the truck and rolled out a moving blanket. She was clearly excited. Chloe and Evie headed into the locker and Maddie watched her sisters with indulgence.

"Aren't you going to get into this action?" Aiden asked.

"Nah. Luckily, Zoe's excited enough for everyone, and I have pretty much everything I need."

"What are you going to do with the money you get from your Grandmother's estate?" he asked.

"That'll go into a savings account."

"Maddie, there's an orange floor lamp. Do you want this, or can we take it?" Zoe shouted.

"Please say you want it," Chloe begged.

"It's all yours." Maddie shuddered.

Aiden must have blocked the memory of the orange floor lamp. Thank God his woman had good taste in clothes. He looked at her bent over in a pink halter top and white capris and made sure his expression stayed neutral. It wouldn't gain him any points if her sisters saw him ogling her.

"Okay, start telling me what needs to be put onto the truck," he ordered.

"I've got this lamp," Zoe said.

"And this mirror," Chloe pointed to something buried in bubble wrap. At least Evie's bosses had done a good job packing her stuff.

Aiden assessed the contents of the locker. Most of the furniture would fit in the truck if it was packed correctly.

"Girls, who's going to help you unload the truck?"

"Clive and Henry and a couple of other guys. We're buying them pizza."

"Who's Henry?" Maddie asked.

"He's Clive's brother. Zoe likes him better, but he doesn't even know she exists. It's complicated," Chloe explained.

"Zoe, don't get pushed into going out with Clive if you don't want to," Maddie said worriedly. "Do you want me to come up to ETSU with you?"

Aiden smiled. He was really beginning to like Maddie. She had a lot of Evie's protective instincts.

"I don't want you driving that truck back to the university with it loaded up. It'll be too unwieldy," Aiden said. "I'll drive it, and the three of you can follow in the rental car and have time to catch up with one another. When we get there, I can introduce myself to Clive and Henry."

"Thanks, Handsome! That's a great idea," Evie said enthusiastically.

"Are you going to go all Drake on them?" Zoe asked suspiciously.

"He's worse than Drake," Evie said. "He goes all icy. If they're assholes, he'll freeze them into the ground. They'll run for the hills. This Clive guy sounds like he could be an asshole."

"Nah," Zoe started.

"He definitely has asshole tendencies," Chloe said.

"His truck shouts asshole," Maddie concurred. "There is now an asshole free zone for Avery girls, are we clear Zoe?"

"He's really hot," Zoe wheedled. "And anyway, it's just one date."

"There's a nutsack hanging from the trailer hitch," Evie said with exasperation.

"Okay, we'll let Aiden talk to him. If he can't look him in the eye, I won't go out on the date."

"Deal," Evie said.

* * *

"The twins are a riot," Aiden said as he got into bed beside Evie at the hotel.

She smiled. It was true, the twins were a handful, they always had been.

"What did you think of Maddie?"

"She took me by surprise." Aiden pushed one of his pillows over to her so she could sleep more comfortably.

"How did she surprise you?"

"Come closer, and I'll tell you."

Snuggling up to Aiden was no hardship. She breathed in his scent and smiled. "Spill it."

"She wanted to make sure I wouldn't hurt you again."

That had her head jerking up. She knew Maddie would be concerned, but actually confronting Aiden would have been tough for her.

"What did she say?"

"She told me how special you are, and she wanted my promise that I would take care of you. You hold a special place in her heart."

"So you got to see what she is really like? You could see that she is really rare."

"Yes, Kitten, Maddie is just as wonderful as you told me." He traced her jaw with his fingertips. "You hit the sister jackpot."

"I did, didn't I?" She grinned. Then her voice lowered. "Do you want to know something else?"

"Sure."

"My boyfriend doesn't have stripper mud flaps on his SUV, so I hit the jackpot there, too."

"Really?" he whispered. "Then I think you should reward him."

"Do you have an idea of what he might like?"

Aiden bent down and whispered in her ear.

Chapter Nineteen

Aiden was smiling a week later when he heard from Dex that the sale of the hotel had finally gone through. It had taken longer than he'd wanted, but still, it had happened. The police hadn't found the person responsible for the break-in, and neither had the private detective that Aiden had hired.

"Do you want him to continue to look?" Dex asked.

Aiden thought about it. "Does he have any leads?"

"He's chasing down a lead on the C-4 that was used to open up the safe."

"Okay, then have him continue," Aiden answered. "Thanks, Dex."

"I'm not done. Lydia did a great job with clearing up the picture of the English- speaking dude in Turkey. We handed that to Interpol. They're putting him through their databases as we speak."

That was great news. "Thanks again. I'll call Lydia."

"So when are you coming back to the *good* SEAL team? Now that you've got a woman, is there really any reason for you to stay with Midnight Delta?"

Aiden barked out a laugh. "Do the men really talk about Midnight Delta like that?"

"Fuck yeah. It's all over base that your motto isn't 'The Only Easy Day is Yesterday'."

"Okay, I'll bite, what's Midnight Delta's motto?"

"'Happily Ever After is Possible.'"

"Fuck me," Aiden groaned. "Mason hasn't heard that, has he?"

"I think somebody is having a banner made that they plan to put on Drake's truck."

"Holy Hell. Please, Dex, you've got to tell me when they're going to do that. I have to be there."

Then something clicked. "Goddammit. This is all your damned idea, isn't it?"

Dexter Evans was silent.

"Seriously, Aiden, when are you coming back to Black Dawn? Gray said it was only three missions."

"One more, then I'm coming back."

"Okay, if not, then the banner is going on your SUV."

Aiden grinned. He missed his team. "As soon as I come back to Black Dawn, you're going to need to begin your rotation onto Midnight Delta. I think you need a love life."

"Bite your tongue."

Aiden laughed.

* * *

Evie was poring over paperwork from local community colleges. She wanted to start there, and then eventually transfer credits to a university. Aiden took that time to return Rylie's call.

"Huey and the former sheriff are going to be transferred to Angola."

It took a moment for Aiden to catch onto what Rylie was saying. "That's Louisiana's prison. They won't take them, all of their offenses were in Tennessee."

"There have been changes in their records. They'll both be transferred next week."

Aiden thought about what he knew about that prison. Hell, it was known as the Alcatraz of the South. It was one of the worst prisons in the US. For a split second he was happy, but then he thought about the reason that Rylie would have gone to such lengths.

"What did you find?" he asked hoarsely.

"It's gone. In a couple of cases I was able to backtrack the content on the websites to peoples' personal computers. We have the feds on their asses."

"We?"

Rylie sighed. "Most of this I was able to handle on my own. Anything that dealt with Evie's pictures was just me," she rushed to assure him.

Aiden waited.

"But when I wanted to trace back to these fucker's computers I needed help. I grabbed a friend. He's solid. He just knew that we were dealing with some underage pornography. We'd worked sex trafficking in the past, he doesn't know that this is a personal case."

Aiden rolled that information around in his head. He liked it, and so would Evie. It meant that more people would be prosecuted.

"And the web-crawler software?"

"I've got it set up."

Aiden nodded.

"Thanks, Rylie." Then he asked a question he'd been wrestling with. "Do you think Evie would be comfortable knowing it was you who worked on this?"

"You tell her it's me. We've met the one time when she was in the hospital, and another time over at Drake and Karen's apartment. She and I'll have drinks some time and we'll have a heart to heart. We're part of a sisterhood that goes deep. It's all good."

Aiden couldn't believe how lucky he'd gotten when he'd signed on with Midnight Delta. Not just finding Evie, but the men he worked with and their women. All of them were extremely special.

* * *

Aiden walked into his office, and saw Evie with her long hair in a high ponytail. He wondered if she had worn it like that when she was sixteen.

"Kitten, do you have a minute?"

"Sure, what's up?" She set down her pen and smiled up at him.

He tipped his head, "why don't we go out to the deck."

"Okay."

While they watched the setting sun, he told her what he had done. Finally he asked her if she had any questions.

"Angola? Wasn't that the prison from 'Dead Man Walking?'" she asked, referring to a movie they had watched together.

Aiden nodded.

"It looked really bad," she breathed. "Rylie must have been pissed at what she'd found."

"She was."

"She seems so nice, but Drake talked about her once. He said she was a ball-buster. She went after an entire human trafficking ring all on her own."

Aiden had heard the story. Darius Stanton was extremely laid-back, except when someone brought up his fiancée's antics, then all bets were off.

"I heard about that, too."

Evie's fingers twisted with his. "What is it, Kitten?"

"If she was mad enough to have Huey and the sheriff transferred from Tennessee to Louisiana, then it must have been a lot worse then I remembered. The pictures I mean." She had squeezed her fingers so tight that they were bloodless.

"Honey, she didn't say anything about that. She has a younger sister who's about the same age as you were when the pictures were taken."

"Oh, yeah." She released his hand. "I forgot."

He pulled the scrunchie holding her hair, and ran his fingers through the dark mass, massaging her scalp.

"That feels good," her voice was thick.

"I'm glad."

"Not the massage. It feels good knowing that this is finally behind me," her voice shook.

"I know, Kitten."

"Thank you for calling Rylie. I've got to call and thank her."

"She said something about you two going out for drinks."

"I'd like that."

She twisted in his hold so she could stare up at him. "You continue to be my hero."

* * *

Evie was happy to see Maddie's number pop up on her phone. She could always use a break from housework.

"Hey, Mads. How's everything going? I warned you not to take the blender, it was a piece of shit. But no backsies."

"That's not why I'm calling. Trenda said you were putting all your eggs in the math and sciences basket. I was calling to remind you about the book report you helped me with."

"What are you talking about? What report?"

"*To Kill a Mockingbird*. Don't you remember?"

Evie searched her memory and came up empty.

"Nope." Evie stopped wiping the kitchen counter, took the phone off speaker and put it up to her ear. "Seriously, I don't know what you're talking about."

"I'm not surprised you don't remember. I was sick the week the report was due, you read the book one night, and wrote the report for me the next day. I got an 'A'."

"You're lying to me. I don't remember that at all."

"Really? You read the book while you were working at the LeeHy motel. You told me that it was a distraction from making beds. Does that ring a bell?"

Suddenly Evie remembered the paperback book that she'd read at the motel. There had been the two kids, Boo, and their dad Atticus. Everything came roaring back. How could she have ever forgotten that book? At the time it had seemed like a parallel of her life, another example of Southern injustice.

And there it was. After she had written Maddie's report, she had balled up those feelings from the book and pressed them deep down in her psyche so she wouldn't have to think about them ever again. So she wouldn't be reminded about Drake being forced to leave town, Dad almost killing Piper, and what Huey and the sheriff had done.

"Evie, are you listening to me?"

"Yes, I'm listening."

"Mr. Roark loved that report. He said I had real promise as a writer. He was really impressed with my ability to relate to the characters. Evie, you need to major in English."

She heard a click on the phone.

"Hold on, I've got another call coming in."

Evie waited, thinking about what Maddie had said. She'd totally blocked that memory. Now that Maddie was telling her about it, she remembered how pleased she'd been to read the notes from Maddie's teacher. But a year later she found herself struggling to pass the GED classes. She'd been so tired. Maybe she'd been selling herself short.

"I'm back," Maddie said.

"That was fast."

"People must think we're stupid. I swear, do they really think we're going to give out a bunch of personal information over the phone? This is the fifth time in the last three weeks. This time I finally blocked him. I should have done it sooner."

"Good for you. I hate that shit. So what can I nag you about? Are your classes going well? Are you dating?"

"Classes are great, and you know damn well that I'm not dating."

"Mads, come on, you're going to have to eventually try again. That one guy was a bastard, but there are good guys. You have to put yourself out there to find one."

"I don't want to talk about it, okay?"

"Okay," Evie sighed. "Thanks for jogging my memory about the book report."

"No problem."

"Have you talked to the others?"

"I babysat Bella the other day while Trenda went to Knoxville to see a client. She got the contract, she's pretty excited. It was weird seeing her in a business suit. She's going to knock their socks off."

"She's such a great graphic designer," Evie enthused.

"I always thought she should do web design," Maddie said.

"Nah, that's too techie for Trenda. Anyway, she'd be on-call more often if she had to support the websites, and then she wouldn't have the schedule flexibility that she has right now. Nope, this is perfect for her."

"Yeah, I see what you mean," Maddie agreed. "Here's the scoop on the twins. Chloe is focused on school, Zoe is focused on getting a part time job."

"Why the hell is Zoe getting a part time job? For God's sake, she's getting a check in a month."

Maddie giggled.

"Holy Hell, it's a guy, right?" Evie guessed.

"Nope, it's guys plural. The fire department is putting together a fundraiser, and they needed someone to help coordinate it. The job doesn't pay. Zoe is competing with thirty other co-eds."

Evie rolled her eyes. "So Clive is off the radar."

"She's on *his* radar, she says he doesn't register on her radar. Personally I think she's lying to herself."

"Does Trenda know about the fire department job?" Evie asked.

"I'm sure as hell not going to tell her," Maddie responded.

"Zoe is going to be the death of her."

"She's going to be the death of all of us," Maddie laughed.

* * *

Aiden had known that this would eventually happen. He drove up to the house and thought about how he was going to break the news to Evie. Of course, she'd known that his job required him to be gone at different times, it's just that this was the first time they'd had to deal with it. He parked the SUV and went inside and was immediately assailed with the scent of salmon.

"Hi, Handsome! You're right on time," Evie called from the kitchen. "Take a load off, and I'll get the table set."

"Do I have time for a quick shower?"

"Absolutely."

When he got to the bedroom he noted '*To Kill A Mockingbird'* on the nightstand. She'd cried last night as she'd read some of it. She'd told him what part of the book she was reading, and he remembered talking to his mom about it when he was reading it in high school.

That was one of the best things Evie had done for him, she had brought his parents back into the light. He could now think of the happy times with them. When he was under the spray of the shower, he heard a noise. He looked up and saw Evie standing there with a beer in her hands.

He turned off the water, and stepped out of the shower, and reached for a towel to dry off. "Whatcha doing?"

"Bringing my man a beer."

"Thank you, Kitten. You didn't have to."

"It had the side benefit of letting me ogle your naked body."

He laughed.

"You think I'm kidding. I'm not. I really like looking at you," she said softly.

His face heated. She grabbed the towel out of his hands and stared at him. It should have embarrassed him, but how could it when he felt the exact same way about her?

"Put the beer down, Eva."

She set the bottle down on the bathroom counter.

"Will you strip for me?" He monitored her reaction. He didn't want to bring up any bad memories. If her sultry smile was anything to go by, she was just fine with his suggestion.

"The salmon's ready," she protested.

"We can reheat it. Take off your clothes." She unbuttoned her blouse slowly, looking up at him from beneath her lashes. She let the cotton fall to the floor. She was wearing a delicate peach bra with a front clasp. She took her time unfastening it, until finally the cups fell forward, and his mouth watered as her pretty pink breasts were revealed. She smiled at him knowingly.

Evie seemed to get into the program, because she slid her right hand down the front of her stomach until it reached the button of her jeans, then she popped it open. Slowly she unzipped the denim, but she didn't start taking off her pants, instead she pushed her hand inside the front panel of her panties.

Game over.

In two strides he picked her up and carried her into the bedroom.

"I wasn't done," she softly protested.

"Oh, you were done all right," he said as he followed her down onto the bed. His lips covered hers. She welcomed him, and he devoured her.

He knelt up and pulled her jeans off.

"Yes, now." She rolled towards the nightstand, but he wasn't done with her yet.

He slowly shook his head and she shuddered. He parted her legs and realized that her little strip tease had left her wet and wanting. He positioned her thighs over his shoulders.

"No Aiden, I need you inside me."

He chuckled, just before he speared his tongue deep. She moaned. It was so good. There wasn't a part of her that wasn't made for him. He took his time, driving her higher, listening to her sounds, and feeling the flutter of her delicate muscles. When she was at the precipice, he stopped and lunged for the condom.

"God, yes," she cried as he drove inside her. She came apart in his arms.

* * *

The salmon ended up being beyond repair, not that either of them cared. They fixed themselves peanut butter and jelly sandwiches. They were eating cross-legged on the floor in the living room.

"Kitten, I need to talk to you."

"You have your serious voice going on," she said as she dunked the last bit of her sandwich in her grape juice.

"We're being deployed tomorrow morning. I have to leave at oh-three hundred."

She kept her hand steady as she finished off the last bite. She was proud of that.

"Do I get to ask you where you're going?"

He shook his head. "Nothing. Not where I'm going or how long I'm going to be gone. Nothing. I might, or might not be able to phone."

Evie gulped down the rest of her juice. They'd talked about this, of course they had. But now that she was faced with it, it had come too soon. She wiped her mouth with the paper towel, her mind racing.

"You need to get to bed. You need your beauty sleep. And this isn't a good enough dinner. Do you need help packing?" She was babbling.

"Eva, it's going to be all right." He picked the dishes up off the floor and put them on the coffee table.

She nodded, letting her hair fall over her face. He was too good for that. He pushed it back so he could see her eyes.

"I've been doing this for sixteen years. I'm good."

"You have scars." He did. There were two bullet wounds and a knife wound.

"That was from when I was younger. I'm older and wiser."

"You probably move slower now," she mumbled.

"The other guys on the team are younger, I'll hide behind them," he teased.

"Sure, I believe in the Easter bunny, too."

"Kitten, this is what I do." He cupped her face. "I'm seriously good at my job. If they didn't think I was, they'd put me behind a desk."

She searched his deep blue eyes and took comfort in what she saw.

"Okay, but you need your rest, and have something better to eat than a PB&J."

"Let's go to bed, and you can make me a good breakfast."

"Ewww, I have to get up that early?" she complained teasingly as they got up off the floor.

He smacked her ass. "Some girlfriend you are."

"Hey, you liked my strip tease."

"I surely did, and I want another one when I get home."

"Deal."

Chapter Twenty

Aiden and Drake had been gone for a week and a half. She had only heard from Aiden once. Luckily time wasn't dragging by. She had finished her applications to three different community colleges, two of them really close by. Today she was headed over to Karen and Drake's apartment to pick up Karen's mother. She'd invited Mrs. Eastman to stay in one of the rooms at her and Aiden's house for the next four days while she was helping Karen plan the Christmas wedding.

As she was grabbing the keys to the SUV off the kitchen counter, her phone rang. It was Zoe.

She was immediately met with swearing. "Calm down. I can't understand what you're saying."

"I think my identity was hacked, or stolen, or something," Zoe wailed.

"What?"

"Yeah, I went to the car dealership and they had no record of me. I thought I was going to get a car, and they didn't have any of my information. What am I going to do?"

"Honey, calm down. What does a car dealership have to do with anything?"

"I tried to buy a car or course."

Evie felt a headache of mammoth proportions start coming on. "What does that have to do with your identity being stolen?"

"Trenda already lectured me. Somebody tried to pull the same scam on her, but she just blocked them. But after she was done, she said I should call you. She said you have freaky computer guys who could maybe help me."

It was like trying to nail Jell-O to the wall, or herding cats.

"Zoe Ann Avery. Listen to my question. Why did you go to the car dealership?"

"Some guy called me up. This is the fourth time he called from the dealership, and this time I filled out the application over the phone because he had the car I wanted. He was really trustworthy. I swear it. He had an English accent and everything."

"Oh, Zoe, what were you thinking."

"Evie, I was cautious, honest. I only gave him my email address the second time, and he sent me pictures of cars. See, I was good."

She didn't rail at her young sister like she wanted to.

"Can you help me? Was Trenda right? Do you have some people who can help?"

"Let me make a few calls. But, Sweetie, you know you might just have to close down all of your accounts, and put fraud alerts on your credit cards, right?"

"Will that take care of me?"

"I don't know. Let me talk to Dex."

"Thank you, thank you, thank you. You're the bestest sister in the whole universe!"

Evie hung up the phone and called Karen to say she would be late picking up her mother.

"That's all right. We decided to order in Chinese food. We were going to call you and ask what you wanted,"

Evie explained what was going on.

"You know, you might want to call Lydia Hildalgo. She might appreciate something to keep her mind off Clint being out on that mission with Drake and Aiden."

"Do you have her number?" Evie asked.

"Let me get it for you."

* * *

Evie had met Lydia once before. She and Clint had come to see her soon after she was brought home from Turkey. Drake and Aiden had explained how she, Dex and Clint had worked together to rescue her.

This time she went over to Lydia and Clint's townhome and she was blown away with all of the computer equipment. "No wonder Karen said you might be able to help Zoe."

Lydia had her sit down in front of a bank of monitors. "I can't access items on your sister's phone, only the phone records associated with your sister's device. Does that make sense?"

Evie nodded.

"So I tracked the phone number that made the calls. There were plenty of calls, made to Zoe, but only four actual pick-ups. I then did a search on the number. It's a disposable phone, that was just recently purchased at Wal-Mart in Tennessee. It doesn't have a real calling plan, instead they're using purchased minutes. But I found something interesting. They've made calls to only seven numbers, five of which are good, two of which are out of service."

"How did you do that so fast?" Evie asked.

Lydia motioned to the computers. Evie nodded. Lydia could probably hack into the Bank of China with this set-up.

"But hold on, this is important. The calls went to, Jim Evans, Blake Tenkins, and your five sisters."

"Holy Fuck!"

"Exactly, we've got a problem. Can you think how they all trace back to you?"

Evie's brain raced. *Think, Avery, think!*

She pulled her phone out of her purse and looked at it.

"All of those numbers were in my cell phone, the one I had in Turkey."

"Do you know what happened to that phone?"

Evie thought back to the room she was in when she was rescued. They'd found her fanny pack, but it'd been empty.

"They used my phone to make the calls to Jim, and send the videos. It was the man with the English accent who had it." She stared at Lydia, aghast. "Zoe said that the man who took her information over the phone had an English accent."

"Holy Fuck," Lydia breathed. "Call Zoe. Now!"

Evie fumbled then dropped her phone when she went to call Zoe.

"Dammit," she said as she picked it up off the floor.

"Take a breath," Lydia advised. Evie pulled in a deep one, then hit Zoe's number on her phone. She got voicemail. "Zoe, call me. It's important." She then sent her a text. Next she called Chloe. It went to voicemail. She checked her watch. It was after school for them, where were they? Hell, Zoe had called only two hours ago, how had she managed to disappear already?

She called Trenda next.

In the background, she could hear Lydia placing a call to Clint. She felt a lot better knowing that Clint would be talking to Aiden and Drake. That is, if they were allowed to pick up messages.

"Hi, Baby Girl," Trenda answered the phone.

"Where's Zoe?" Evie asked urgently.

"She's probably at her place."

"The man from Turkey who kidnapped me, is the man who's been making the phone calls to all of you. He has Zoe's address and information. She's a target. Where is she?"

"She could be anyplace."

"What about Chloe?" Evie asked.

"She's probably with Zoe," Trenda answered.

"Where's Maddie?"

"At home. I'll call her." Trenda said.

"Trenda, you need to leave your house. He could have found out where you live. If he found Chloe and Zoe's address, he could have found you. You need to bail now. I'll call Maddie."

"Are you sure this is the same guy?" Trenda asked urgently.

"I'm sure. Get out of the house now!"

"What does he want?"

"Don't ask questions. Get. Out. Of. Your. House!" Evie hung up and called Maddie. She was barely keeping it together.

In the background she heard Lydia's phone ring. Please, God , say it was Clint.

Maddie picked up on the first ring. "Hi, Evie, I was just going to call you. Great minds. How is '*To Kill A-*"

"Maddie, you need to leave your apartment."

"I'm not at my apartment. I'm at Starbucks."

"Don't go back to your apartment. The guy who kidnapped me is in Tennessee. He knows where the twins live. He could know where you and Trenda live. I'm going to be there as soon as I can."

"What the hell are you talking about?"

"The guy never got the passports he wanted. They're worth millions. Jim's friend needed to get them. The only thing this man has to lead him to the passports is my old phone. He's been trying to get ahold of Jim and Blake but Aiden made them change their numbers and totally disappear, that leaves y'all. He's going to try to take one of you to get to me."

"That's crazy!"

"No it's not. It's desperate."

"That means you can't come to Tennessee. We need to get the authorities involved."

Evie bit her thumbnail. Maddie was right. "Just don't go home. Can you try to get ahold of Zoe and Chloe? I'm going to get ahold of Piper and make sure she never talked to this asshole. Thank God you blocked him."

"I'll have them call you as soon as I get ahold of either Zoe or Chloe."

"Thank you."

She hung up and turned to Lydia. "Was that Clint?"

"Yep. The guys are two hours from Coronado. They were planning on surprising us."

"Woohoo, surprise," Evie said wanly. "I need to call Piper and make sure she didn't talk to him."

"It's going to be all right."

"You've already said that." Evie reminded the woman. " But, there's a madman after my sisters."

"We're going to stop him. He's not going to touch them. I promise."

"The guys aren't here."

"We don't need them," Lydia said as she turned to her computer. Evie looked at her in amazement. Holy hell, she was totally sincere.

She punched in Piper's number. Fuck, it went to voicemail.

* * *

Where Drake was animated rage, Aiden was silent ice.

"Lydia already has our tickets out of San Diego. She and Evie are going to be there three hours sooner than we are because they're leaving out of LAX," Clint informed the Midnight Delta team.

Aiden had already had a futile conversation with Evie, she was going with Lydia to Tennessee. Evie was hell on wheels on a good day, but add Lydia into the mix and she thought she could conquer the world. What was with these women?

"Clint, can't you get Lydia to stand down?" Aiden demanded.

"What would be the fun in that?" Clint laughed. "But seriously, it will be good for them to get there as soon as possible. Lydia has our contacts at homeland security, she'll coordinate with them."

"I hear a but in that statement."

"She already reached out. There not putting a lot of credence in Evie's claim that her kidnapper from Turkey is in Tennessee, so I don't know how much help we're going to get. They aren't going to get there until later tonight."

"Aiden, what's the chance that this guy is acting alone?" Mason asked.

"Slim to none, he's a recruiter for his organization."

"If his end game is to get the passports, why target Evie's sisters?" Jack asked.

"Her phone and the email address were the only two things he had left to connect him to the passports. Dex shut down the email address, so he must be thinking to take one of Evie's sisters as leverage to force Nathan to hand over the passports."

"Do we know where Nathan is?" Mason asked.

"We left his ass to RLI to deal with. He'd fucked up the whole project and you know those mercenaries won't let it stand. If I had to guess, he's probably six feet under," Clint answered. "Right now the CIA and Interpol are working to get the passports."

"Who has contacts with the CIA?" Mason asked.

"Gray does," Aiden answered. "I'll have him find out if they're anywhere close to finding the passports."

"Lydia's been coordinating with Interpol," Clint added.

Aiden turned when Drake's hand slammed against the wall of the ship. "When are they letting us off?"

"We have priority. Twenty minutes at the max," Mason assured Drake.

Gray was waiting for them at the dock to take them straight to the airport. The problem was their flight had a layover, that's why the women would be there so much sooner than they would.

Jack and Dare had to stay behind to debrief the Captain. Normally Mason would leave Clint to do it, but there was no way he would remain behind while Lydia was in Tennessee.

* * *

As soon as the flight attendant said it was safe to turn on the cell phone, Lydia and Evie had theirs out.

"Lydia, should my sister's even have their phones on? Can that bastard locate them, like we located him?"

"No Evie, if he could have done that, he wouldn't have been calling each of them to find out their information over the phone."

"Fuck, I'm so stupid."

"No, you're right to be thinking of all the angles." Lydia covered her hand. "Now call your sisters and find out where they are."

Lydia and Evie were sitting near the back of the plane, so they had time to make calls. She heard Lydia calling Dex, but then Trenda's phone connected. Bella answered. "Hello?"

"Hello, Baby. It's Aunt Evie. Can I talk to your Mama?"

"We're at the LeeLee notel Aunt Evie. We can get cans of pop from the machine."

"That's great. Can you give your Mama the phone?"

"Mama! Aunt Evie's on the phone."

"Darn it all. Isabella, I told you not to play with Mommy's phone." Trenda got on the line. "Evie, are you all right? Where are you?"

"*I'm* fine. Where are *you*?"

"I'm over at the LeeHy motel."

"That rat trap?"

"It was close and I could get a room. Nobody's going to find me here. Relax."

"Why didn't you go stay at one of the resort hotels?"

"It's the Thursday before Labor Day weekend, they're all booked up."

"Okay, keep your head down, Trenda.

"You got it, what are you going to do?"

"Lydia and I are heading over to Chloe and Zoe's place."

"Aren't you going to call the police?"

"Lydia's got someone who is coming to Jasper Creek who will be meeting us. They will be here soon."

"What is soon?"

"Soon," Evie stalled, wanting to end that line of questioning. From what Lydia said they weren't going to arrive for a couple of more hours. The men would probably arrive first. "Just trust us. Do you know where Maddie is?"

"She's been hanging out at the Polly's Restaurant. She just commandeered a booth, plugged in her laptop and made herself at home. She's going to spend the night here with me and Bella."

Evie could see why Maddie might not want to spend the day there.

Okay, so three of her sisters were accounted for when she included Piper who was safe in California. She'd gotten the phone calls, but she just had a policy of never answering calls that she didn't recognize. She'd need to give lessons to Zoe when this was over with.

It was their turn to get up. They didn't have any carry-on items, everything was at baggage claim. Lydia had wanted to take a gun. When Evie had asked for one, Lydia asked her if she knew how to handle one, and Evie had to admit that she didn't.

"Then you don't get one. A gun in the hands of someone not trained is worse than not having one." Evie trusted Lydia, so she didn't balk, especially when she saw how competent the woman was in handling it.

At baggage claim she tried to get ahold of either Chloe or Zoe once again. No luck.

Shit!

She had her phone up to her ear as she followed Lydia to the rental car counter. "Maddie?"

"Are you here? Do you need a ride?"

"No, we're renting a car and heading over to their apartment at ETSU right now. I wish we could get one of them on the phone so we didn't have to make the drive."

"I've texted and emailed them. Nada! Nothing! I can believe it from Zoe, but not Chloe. This is so unlike her. Maybe it's because it's almost Labor Day weekend?" Maddie said thoughtfully.

"I don't care why it is, they need to answer. Just keep at it, will you?"

"You got it."

CHAPTER TWENTY-ONE

All of the men were too big to sit comfortably in commercial, and to make matters worse, because they hadn't gotten reservations ahead of time, they were all in middle seats. Aiden kept his eyes closed during the majority of the trip from Dallas to Tennessee, trying to work out all of the angles of their upcoming mission.

Lydia had called Clint from the Tennessee airport and left a message updating him to say they were on their way to the twins' apartment at ETSU.

Aiden had called Dex during their short layover in Dallas. Dex had come through with some information from Interpol. They had identified the man with the English accent. His name was Khalid Clifford. He was born in Belgium and educated in England. He had travelled extensively in the Middle East and was known as a recruiter for the cause. That would be why he wanted to get his hands on passports, he would want his minions to have access to countries across Europe and even into the United States.

"Dex, does Interpol show he's in the US?" Aiden asked.

"Yep. Landed about a week before the hotel was broken into."

"So he's had plenty of time to recruit people to help him," Aiden bit out.

"That's my take," Dex agreed.

"Do you have any good news?"

"Yes. Clint has a tracking device on his phone for Lydia, and I've installed one for Evie on yours."

"That is good news!"

"I have two trucks waiting for you at the rental counter when you get there. Call me when you land. I might have more information then."

"You got it."

* * *

It took them an hour and a half to get to the girl's apartment.

"It's a nice area," Lydia commented.

Evie was too keyed up to care. She'd been driving like a bat out of hell, and, luckily they hadn't been pulled over. She'd made Lydia call her sister's number every fifteen minutes, but nobody answered.

She parked on the street, and jumped out of the car.

"Whoa. We can't go off half-cocked. You're the one they want Evie. You need to stay in the car, and let me go up to the door like I'm just one of their friends."

"You think he has them?"

"No, not really."

"Why not?"

"Because he would have already called your cell phone with them on it."

Bile rose, she thought she would throw up, for just a moment she was back in that room, the man pointing her pink phone at her.

"How could I have not realized?" Evie's voice was hoarse.

"Don't beat yourself up. It's good news, but we need to be smart about this and let me go knock on the door."

Evie nodded. Lydia walked calmly up the walk towards the apartment that Chloe and Zoe shared. Evie watched as she knocked on the door, and then she saw how it pushed open. Lydia disappeared inside. She looked down at her watch, if Lydia was gone for more than ninety seconds, she was going in after her.

Sixty seconds after she went in, she came out and waved at Evie. She shot out of the car. Lydia stopped her before she went into the apartment. "It's a shambles, but there's no sign of a struggle, so that's good."

She went inside, and the first thing she saw is the huge chalkboard that covered the wall in the dining room. She'd forgotten how artistic Zoe was.

Every drawer was open, the desk that the sisters shared had all of its papers strewn about the floor. The small filing cabinet beside it had been upended. Somebody had been searching for something.

"What were they looking for?"

"My guess is your address."

"Thank God they weren't here, but where are they?" Evie looked around the room, and then the hair on the back of her neck stood up. There on the chalkboard was damn near everything the kidnappers needed.

LABOR DAY WEEKEND AT LACIE'S! CHEROKEE LAKE, HERE WE COME!

She rushed over to the board and saw where there had been something taped to it, but it had been ripped off. She pulled what was left off, and saw part of an invitation.

Oh God.

Oh God.

Oh God.

The kidnappers would know exactly where her sisters were. They were at Cherokee Lake with Lacie Danvers. She remembered the girl, but she had no idea where the house might be. She needed to call Maddie.

Maddie didn't say hello when she answered, she just asked if Evie and Lydia had found the twins.

"No. But we know where they went. There was an invitation for them to go to Cherokee Lake with Lacie Danvers. Do you know where her house is?"

"It's her uncle's cabin. I've been there once, but I have no idea how to tell you to get there."

Evie had it on speaker and Lydia was listening in.

"Maddie, this is Lydia. What's Lacie's uncle's name? I can get the records and get the address."

"Oh shit. It's not really her uncle. He's a friend of the family, and I don't know him except as Uncle Walt. I was there once. If you pick me up I'm sure I can get us there."

"No. We don't need any more innocents involved." Lydia's tone was emphatic. Evie touched her arm. She looked at the woman's strained face. She remembered that she was an older sister, too.

"Lydia, we have no choice. Cherokee Lake is just too big for us to go out there alone without some idea of where we're going. We need Maddie."

"Pick me up at Polly's. I'll be ready to go."

* * *

"I should drive." Maddie said as she ran up to the SUV. She had a duffle bag swinging in her arms.

Lydia was already in the backseat, and Evie pointed to the passenger seat.

"But I know where-"

"Seriously Mads, don't give me any shit. We know who the better driver is. You navigate, I drive. We don't have time."

Maddie shut up, got in and buckled up. She tossed the bag over the seat.

"I'm sorry, I didn't mean to be a bitch."

"You weren't. But I was just trying to help. I brought back-up."

"What do you mean?" Evie asked.

"Polly's daughter is on a softball team. That's her bat-bag," she said gesturing to the duffle bag she'd just thrown into the back seat.

"You're amazing. Do you hear that Lydia? My sister gave me a weapon. You might not have given me a gun, but I damn well have a bat to play with!"

Maddie's head whipped around to the back seat. "You have a gun?"

Lydia nodded. She was staring out the window. "How far away is the lake from here?"

"It's an hour's drive. The last twenty minutes is backroads."

"How sure are you that you can find this place, Maddie?" Evie asked.

"We might take a couple of wrong turns, but I'll get us there eventually."

"Lydia, are you going to be able to write down the directions so you can give them to Clint and Aiden?" Evie asked.

"No need."

"Huh?" Evie glanced at her in the rearview mirror.

Lydia held up her phone. "GPS. Clint has me tracked. He'll be able to pinpoint our location. He'll find us."

The amount of relief Evie felt was ridiculous. So much for always wanting to handle things on her own.

"They will have landed by the time we have arrived at the lake," Lydia said.

Evie took a deep breath. Yeah, she was relieved that Aiden was going to be here. She needed him. But, he was going to be so pissed.

"Clint is going to hand me my ass."

Evie looked at Lydia in the backseat and saw her wearing a shit-eating grin. It sparked a small smile on her own face. She wanted to take this fucker down, didn't she? Damn right she did. And she had a bat to do it with.

* * *

The four men were at baggage claim, Clint was repeating back what Lydia was saying to him on the phone.

"They've gone to a lake. It's in the middle of bumfuck nowhere. Lydia says that there having a hell of a time finding the right place, so hopefully our target is having problems finding it too."

"What the fuck?" Drake said.

Aiden had already tried to call Evie, but it went to voicemail.

"Clint, why can you talk to Lydia, and I can't talk to Evie?" he demanded.

"My woman has a satellite phone. Yeah it's overboard, but what can I say, anything less freaks me the hell out."

Aiden saw Mason and Drake making mental notes to get Sophia and Karen satellite phones in the future. Evie would have one before the weekend was done.

Just then Evie called him back.

"Why didn't you pick up before?" he demanded.

"Aiden? This is Maddie. Evie's driving."

"I want you to pull over to the side of the road and wait for us. We're an hour away from the lake."

"No!" Evie and Lydia said the same word at the same time. Apparently Maddie had the phone on speaker.

"I'm hanging up now," Aiden heard Clint saying in stereo. He was in the girl's car and in the airport with the men. Aiden put his phone on speaker so all of the men could hear what was being said, he didn't give a shit about the rest of the passengers in baggage claim, they'd just have to cope.

"You will pull over. You will wait for us. You will not pass go. You will not collect two hundred dollars." Drake said.

"Fuck you, Drake," Evie yelled.

Aiden saw a mother take her three children and walk to the furthest side of the baggage carousel.

"Guys, keep it together," Mason counseled in a low tone. "We have you tracked. What is your game plan?"

"We're not just going to drive up to the cabin, if that's what you're thinking," Evie said sarcastically.

"Well thank God for small favors," Drake growled.

"Shut it," Aiden snapped. "Evie, tell us your plan."

"Maddie said that there is a cabin right next to Lacie's with a cabin that shares a dock. We're going to go to that cabin, down to the shared dock. Lydia is going to approach from the water, because nobody will recognize her. She's going to pose as the neighbor."

"You promise that's all you're going to do?" Aiden asked.

"I promise," Evie said.

"Lydia, what are you going to do when you get to the cabin?" Clint asked.

"I'm not going to go into the cabin no matter what. You know those give me the creeps, Clint," she promised.

"You still haven't answered my question."

"Clint. You know if they had the girls they would have called Evie by now. They would have been trying to make a move. This is a moot point."

"Humor me. Tell me what you're going to do, Lydia." He was getting angry.

"I've got my gun. I'm going to stay fluid and take them by surprise if I can."

"That's fucking bullshit. You will pull over by the side of the road!"

"I'm sorry, the connection's getting bad. Evie, we must be getting too close to the lake, I think we're losing the men. Clint? Can you hear me?"

"Don't pull this shit, Lydia!"

"Clint? Are you saying something?"

The line went dead.

Drake chuckled.

"Shut up and let's get to the rental car place. I want us at the lake twenty minutes ago." Clint eyed his duffel bag and grabbed it. Aiden was sure that it wasn't an accident when he swung it off the carousel and it hit Drake in the head.

* * *

Evie stared down at her phone and prayed to God it wouldn't ring.

"Lydia, what would happen if the kidnapper couldn't get a connection from the lake when he was trying to reach me?"

"He'd call you from another phone that had a better signal. He wouldn't *not* call you."

Evie relaxed. She knew her phone could pick up calls, because she had received the phone call from Aiden, and despite Lydia's antics, she knew her signal was strong. Still, she prayed with all her might that she wouldn't get a call or, God forbid, a video.

"There it is! I see it! That's the road to Lacie's uncle's cabin."

Evie stomped on the brake and backed up the car.

"Are you sure?"

This was the second time that Maddie had said this.

"Yeah, I recognize this mailbox, it's made in the shape of a trout. I forgot about it before."

Evie took a left down the bumpy road.

"Okay, down to the right is Uncle Walt's place. If we turn down here first it's the Kendall's cabin." Evie took a slow right down an even bumpier dirt road. The place they pulled up to looked like it hadn't seen people in years.

"Okay, if you park here, and we go down that path at the back of the cabin, we'll be at the dock."

The three women got out of the car. Evie stretched, and then pulled the bat bag out of the back seat. She unzipped it and found a blue aluminum softball bat. It had a good heft and felt good in her hands. Maddie bent over the bag and pulled out a gray bat.

"I've been to the batting cages a lot ever since that night," she said softly.

Lydia eyed the two sisters. "You both look kind of scary."

Evie looked at the woman holding the pistol in her hand and laughed. "I think that's our line. Maddie, give her your hoodie. She needs something to wear so that she can hide her gun."

Maddie shrugged out of her hoodie and handed it over to Lydia, who put it on. Evie looked down at her phone again and saw that it was at full signal strength. Still no voicemails, missed calls or videos.

"Eves, we can cut through the woods and blackberry bushes to get to Uncle Walt's. It butts up near their cistern."

"How do you know that?" Evie asked.

"I found Zoe making out underneath it at the last party."

Lydia eyed the two sisters, then nodded. "I'll keep them occupied out back and you can look in the windows on the other side."

"Sounds like a plan," Evie agreed. She palmed her phone. "Is everyone's phone on silence?"

They all nodded.

Evie watched Lydia's curvy figure go down the path towards the dock.

"Who is she? Is she like a cop?"

"She's a bad-ass. Come on, show me the way."

Soon Evie was happy to have the softball bat as she used it to keep the blackberry brambles from scratching the hell out of her face. In the distance she heard Lydia's lilting Spanish accent calling out a loud hello.

They needed to hurry. Finally they nearly fell out of the bushes and into the clearing that housed the water holding tank for Uncle Walt's cabin. For a place that was supposed to be housing a party, it was eerily quiet.

Maddie looked at her, she realized it too. She raised her bat. They could hear Lydia talking, there was the low voice of a man talking. Carefully the two sisters crept up to the sliding glass door, and they saw six girls all lying on the small floor of the living room. For just an instant Evie thought they were all dead. It took a moment for her to process that they were all tied up. A man was crouched over them holding a gun. She could see that the back door was partially open and another man was talking through it. He must be talking to Lydia.

She looked closer at the girls. One of them was Chloe. Where was Zoe? The crouched man wasn't the Englishman. Finally, the man who had been talking to Lydia stepped back into the cabin and shut the door. He turned around and surveyed the girls on the floor. He wasn't the man from Turkey either.

Evie backed away from the sliding glass door.

"Maddie," she said in a barely perceptible whisper.

"What?" she mouthed.

"Switch phones with me and go to the other cabin. Pretend to be me if they call. Also send Lydia back to me. I'll be back to you as quickly as possible."

"I don't understand."

"Just do it."

She watched as Maddie disappeared back through the blackberry bushes. Goddammit, she should have insisted on a gun. What would she do if they started killing the girls? Well, she'd just run with her bat and try to save them. But Lydia better damn well get here fast!

She looked at the time on her phone. Five minutes passed. Then seven. Then nine. Finally, at eleven minutes, Lydia came through the brambles.

It was at that moment that the man who had talked to Lydia grabbed Chloe up by her tied wrists, wrenching her arms. Tears came to Evie's eyes in sympathy as her sister cried out.

Lydia was at her side watching, she put her hand on Evie's shoulder.

"Okay, Cutie, you're going to make us a video," the man said with a Southern accent. "Tell me what your sister's phone number is."

"Never!" Chloe yelled.

The man kicked the girl closest to Chloe, and the girl screamed. In an instant, Chloe wilted. "Please don't hurt my friends."

"Well I guess you're going to do what I say, now aren't you? Aren't you just a lucky little girl that I just want you to say a couple of words on a video? I just have to make you cry a little bit, but nothing too bad. Are you going to give me Evie's telephone number?"

Where was the man who had been with her in Turkey if he wasn't in this cabin? Where was Zoe?

Chapter Twenty-Two

Aiden was in the truck with Clint, whose phone had just rung.

"Lydia, you better not try any funny shit with me again," was how Clint answered the phone. Thankfully he also put it on speaker.

"Hello? This is Maddie, Evie's sister. Is this Aiden?"

"Hi, I'm here Maddie," Aiden answered. "Why are you calling Clint from Lydia's phone?"

"I'm waiting for a call from the kidnapper's to come into Evie's phone. They have Chloe. Lydia and Evie are outside the cabin watching them right now. If they try anything really bad, I think they'll kill them."

"Who'll kill who?" Clint demanded.

"There are six girls tied up in the cabin. If the bad guys try to kill the girls, Evie and Lydia will kill the bad guys. But right now Evie and Lydia are just watching them. I'm supposed to pretend to be Evie and let them video Chloe and call me on Evie's phone. But I'm also supposed to call you from Lydia's phone and tell you to come and find us."

Fuck!

"Okay, Maddie, you're doing good. We can get this done. We'll be there in less than ten minutes. Do you know where Zoe is?"

There was silence.

"Maddie are you still there?" Aiden asked.

"I didn't see her. Oh, God, Aiden, I didn't see her." It was clear the girl was crying.

"Maddie, this is Clint. You're doing really well. You need to keep it together a little longer for when they call you. You need to pretend to be Evie and take that call. You hear me? You need to be brave. You need to take that call and be brave. Can you do that?"

"Yes."

She sounded a little better.

"Good girl, Maddie," Aiden praised her. Then he heard the sound of a FaceTime call coming in.

"I've got to take this."

"Leave this line on. Put us on mute. Can you do that?"

"Yes."

They listened as she answered the call.

"Hello?"

"Is this Evie Avery?"

"Yes."

"We have your sister Chloe. Say hello, Chloe." There was silence. Aiden looked sideways at Clint who was holding his phone in a death grip.

A high pitch screech echoed through the cab of the truck. It took all of Aiden's concentration to stay straight on the road.

"Don't hurt her!" Maddie cried.

"My not hurting her is all up to you."

"Why are you doing this?"

Shit, now came the tricky part, would Maddie know enough to play this part right?

"Just tell me what to do, and I'll do it."

"My boss wants the passports. He says you're the person who can get them. Me? Well, I just want him to be happy, because if he is, I get paid. So here's your incentive to hand over these passports."

Another bone-chilling scream came through the phone.

"Stop!" Maddie yelled. "Please, I'll do anything. Don't hurt her again."

"Get your boyfriends to give my boss the passports. You have three days. Got it?"

"How do I get a hold of you?"

"We'll call you tomorrow."

Aiden looked over at Clint. They didn't want to say anything. The phone should be muted, but just in case it wasn't and just in case he hadn't hung up, they kept silent.

"Did you hear that?" Maddie's voice was clogged with tears.

"You did good, Honey," Aiden said soothingly.

"She screamed! She screamed!" Maddie was screaming.

Aiden glanced over at Clint.

"We're going to get her. She's going to be okay. It's going to be over in just a few more minutes. I promise."

Aiden could hear audible gulps.

"Get here fast. Please get here fast."

"We will."

The line disconnected.

* * *

Evie had somehow kept her gagging silent. She quietly spit out mucus on the ground and wiped her eyes. Lydia's brown eyes were wet with sympathy as she squeezed her arm. Chloe was passed out on the sofa. The man who had hurt her was sitting next to her, his gun resting on the cushion beside him.

If it hadn't been for Lydia, Evie would have gone charging into the cabin, but she had held her back. She'd been right. The two men had two guns and six hostages. The odds were terrible.

"We need a plan," Lydia said softly.

Evie was having trouble thinking.

"You go to the back door this time and distract them."

"I look too much like Chloe."

"By the time they realize that, I'll have come in through the front."

"Are you going to shoot them?"

"Yes," Lydia said levelly.

Evie looked at the woman and realized she was serious.

"One change to the plan."

"What?"

"Maddie will distract them. You and I will go through the front. Two is better than one."

Evie stepped backwards, past the cistern, towards the blackberry bushes, and quietly called Maddie. She told her the plan.

"I'll be there soon. Is Lydia going to kill the men?"

"She's going to shoot them, I don't know if she's going to kill them."

"If she doesn't kill them, you beat the hell out of them with the bat." Maddie then hung up the phone.

Evie walked back to Lydia. They waited. Finally, there was a knock on the back door. Lydia had already checked, the sliding glass door was unlocked. The man on the sofa waved to the other man to open the door. As soon as he began to open it, Evie softly slid open sliding glass door and Lydia slipped in.

One of the girls on the floor saw them, and yelled, "Help!"

The man on the sofa looked up and grabbed his gun. Lydia didn't hesitate, she shot him twice in the chest. He powered backwards against the couch. The sound made the other man turning around. He was beginning to pull his gun out from his shoulder holster while Evie was running past the girls on the floor. She swung the bat high and connected with his cheek. Blood splattered and bone crunched. He fell like a ton of bricks.

* * *

"Turn here!"

Dirt and gravel flew as they went up the drive to the bright yellow cabin. There were a myriad of cars and trucks parked in front of it, and Clint slammed to a stop in front of them. They jumped out of their truck and Aiden heard screaming.

They saw the open sliding glass door and started towards it.

Before they could get to it, Lydia came out pointing a gun.

"What the fuck?!"

"Clint!"

"Put down the gun."

She dropped her arm and took two steps towards him, but before she could go any further he was across the yard and had her in his arms.

"Are you okay, Baby?"

Behind them another truck pulled up and out piled Mason and Drake, both of them with their guns out. Aiden was at the cabin, and saw Maddie and Chloe huddled on the floor, leaning against a couch.

"Aiden, help me." Evie was trying to untie a girl who was struggling. There was another girl who was standing up, and another one who was untying someone else. He saw two more girls tied up and lying on the floor.

"My God," Drake said as he came to a stop inside the cabin. "Chloe!"

"I don't know where Zoe is," she cried thinly.

"We'll find her, Baby Girl." Drake stepped over one of the girls lying on the floor and picked up Chloe. She was covered in blood. "Oh God, we've got to get you to a hospital."

"It's not my blood, Drake."

"Lydia shot the asshole who hit her," Evie said.

Aiden and Mason used their knives to untie the girls. They got them sitting up. "What about this guy?" Mason asked tipping his head towards the bloodied corpse near the door.

"That was Evie hitting another homerun," Maddie said.

Aiden caught sight of the bat on the floor and shuddered. He looked over at Evie. She looked agonized. "Eva?"

"We don't know where Zoe is."

As if she conjured it, a phone rang. "It's your phone. It's a FaceTime call, Evie," Maddie said, holding up the phone.

Everybody turned to where Maddie was standing. Then they relaxed as Maddie grinned. "Oh, don't worry. It's Trenda."

"Don't scare me like that." Evie grabbed the phone from her sister.

She pressed the button to answer, and Aiden watched as her face froze.

"Hello, Evie, do you remember me?" the man with the English accent asked.

Fuck, it was Khalid Clifford.

Evie didn't answer. She just stared at her phone. She looked up at Aiden helplessly.

"Evie, answer the man," he prompted.

Her eyes glossed over with wet, he thought she would burst into tears, but he should have known better.

"Yes I remember you, you asshole. You better not hurt my sister, or I will torch your fucking passports!"

Good for her!

"Do you want to know what I will do to a baby?"

Evie dropped to her knees, but the man on the phone didn't see it, she kept the phone steady in her hands. "For every hair that is harmed on their heads, I will burn a passport. Are we clear?"

"So you *do* have them?"

"I have them," she lied.

"I want them."

"No shit."

"I want them in the next four hours."

"Let me see Trenda and Bella this instant."

Aiden couldn't see what Evie could on the screen but he could see her relieved expression.

"I want my passports."

"I want my sister and niece." Even though she was on her knees, her tone was strong and resolute.

"If you want them alive, it's simple, you just have to give them to me fast enough. Do you see what I have in my hands?"

"Clay?"

"No, my dear, this is C-4. It's an explosive. I'm going to stash your sister and niece in a nice little out of the way place with a little timing device. You'll have four hours to get me my passports. If you fail to get them to me on time, then they will run out of time. That would be too bad because the baby is so cute. I'll call you in an hour to tell you where I want you to deliver the passports."

The phone went dead and Evie dropped it. She slumped over and her body heaved. Aiden was beside her and managed to pull her hair out of the way before she threw up.

"Got him!" Lydia cried.

"Tell us," Mason demanded.

"Aiden, he's going to blow them up," Evie moaned. He gathered her up and tried to listen to Lydia at the same time.

"I had Dex put a trace on the call. Then I had him track Trenda's phone. As long as that asshole has Trenda's phone on him, we know where he's at."

Evie was crying quietly in his arms. She wasn't hearing any of the conversation going on around her.

"Thank fuck!" Drake said. "Now we just have to pick him off before he sets the explosive. Where is he?"

Lydia rattled off an address.

"That's Trenda's house," Maddie said. She crouched down to where Evie was huddled in Aiden's arms. "Evie, you did great. Trenda and Bella are going to be okay. They're at Trenda's house. They're going to rescue them."

Aiden helped Evie lift her head, gratified to see her focus on her sister.

"It's true, Kitten. We're going to get them. You did it."

"Come on Evie. Time to pick up the bat," Lydia said.

* * *

Clint and Aiden were in the front seat of the truck, with Evie and Lydia in the back seat of the cab. Mason and Drake were following right on their tail. For a hot second, Maddie had wanted to go with them, but Drake had said she needed to stay with Chloe and she quickly agreed.

"Left," Lydia said pointing towards a gravel road.

Aiden veered right.

"You're going the wrong way," she cried.

"He isn't baby, look." They all saw the main road ahead.

"Shit, I was going off memory, I should have been looking at the phone's navigation," Lydia said disgustedly.

Now that they were on a paved road, Aiden hit the gas. The landscape blurred by.

"What do we do, since we don't have the passports," Evie asked.

"Doesn't matter," Aiden answered. "We know where they're at. We're going to go get him. Tell us the terrain near Trenda's house."

"It's at the end of the road. The nearest house is probably two hundred yards away, it is surrounded by an empty field on three sides."

"Flat?"

"What do you mean?"

"I mean is the field flat? Does it have trees? Hills? Is there a way to get to the house from the field without being detected?"

Evie thought about it. "About two miles away is Johnson's Dairy Farm. But it's just grassy fields and a couple of fences, there's no rocks or hills." Evie's voice rose with panic. Aiden and Clint looked at one another and grinned.

"It's going to be okay, Evie."

Clint's phone rang and he put it on speaker. Drake's voice filled the cab.

"Did Evie tell you what we're dealing with on the house?" he asked.

"Yeah," Clint answered. "Did you know about the dairy farm?"

"Yes. What's the status on our targets?" Drake asked.

"Don't call them targets," Evie cried out. "That's Trenda and Bella."

"Evie, it's also the kidnapper and whoever else might be there. It's who we're targeting at the house. Your brother isn't being heartless," Aiden soothed, his eyes met hers in the rearview mirror.

Lydia grasped her hand and held it tight.

"Baby Girl, I swear to you, I know who is at that house. I'm going to get them," Drake said.

"I'm sorry, Drake."

"No need. Lydia?" he asked again.

"Dex put Trenda's phone icon in my phone. It's still showing at the same address. As long as he holds onto that, we'll have him."

"That's a big if," Clint said. "I don't like it. He's got to know we'd be tracking that shit."

"That's my take too, Clint." Mason said.

The bottom fell out of Evie's stomach. "If he knows that we know where he is, then what's going on?"

None of the men responded.

"Aiden?" Evie asked.

"It's probably a trap."

"But he wants the passports. I don't understand."

"We'll see what number he calls you from. That'll answer our questions."

* * *

They were on the outskirts of Jasper Creek when Evie got a call from an unknown number. She held it out for Lydia to see.

"Answer it, Evie. You can do this."

"Hello?"

"There's an abandoned Igloo Hut Creamery on Martin Street. I want *you* to put the passports underneath the ice cream cone near the drive thru in a half hour. If it is anybody else but you delivering the passports, the deal is off."

"How do I know you're going to keep your promise and not harm Bella and Trenda?"

"The timer goes off in ninety minutes. Once I have the passports, I'll tell you where they are. I'm sure your erstwhile band of soldiers can disarm the bomb."

Her hand was slick with sweat, and fear permeated her body.

"I want to see them. I want to make sure you haven't hurt them."

He hung up.

Evie burst into tears. Lydia pulled her close.

"You did good, Eva."

"We don't have the passports," she said her voice quaking. "He didn't call from Trenda's phone."

"Evie, we didn't expect him to call from Trenda's phone," Mason said. She'd forgotten they'd been listening in on Clint's phone. God, everything was so confusing. She looked out the window. They were ten minutes away from Trenda's house.

"I'm taking the lead. Follow me," Drake said. Soon both trucks were in the parking lot of the LeeHy motel. All six of them got out. Drake pulled Evie into his arms. "It's going to be okay Baby Girl, we're going to get Trenda and Bella."

Mason was trotting back from the dilapidated lobby carrying an armful of newspapers. Evie watched as he upended his duffle bag, and then pulled out a small gym bag. He yanked out sneakers and gym clothes, then stuffed in the newspapers. Her brain finally kicked in and she realized he had just created something that looked like a bag filled with passports.

"Two-pronged approach?" Aiden asked.

Mason nodded.

"I know the terrain, I'll go to the dairy farm. Clint, you're the ordnance guy, so you're with me. Do we have anything to disarm a bomb?" Drake asked.

Clint's eyes flickered to the duffle bag in the back of the truck. "I have my Swiss Army knife."

Evie didn't moan. Lydia must have seen her expression. She leaned in and whispered in her ear. "That's more than good enough. You'll see."

"Aiden, that leaves you and me for the drop off at the Igloo Hut. We know there's going to be more than just one guy," Mason said.

"I'm looking forward to it. Evie can you tell us about it?"

"It's been closed for over three years, but the drive-thru is still open, kids use it as an obstacle course. It's surrounded by parking spaces, there is no good hiding spots."

"Then it is the perfect place to put on some performance theater," Aiden grinned. He turned to the other men. "Hand me your passports and let's get over to the hardware store."

All four men handed over their passports, and Mason put them into the gym bag.

* * *

Everybody had to play their position. That was the rule of a SEAL team. Aiden knew that Drake and Clint could take care of Trenda and Bella, so now it was up to him and Mason to keep Evie safe. He just hated what he was asking her to do. He watched her through the binoculars. Aiden was hidden up on some crates in the back of a large home goods parking lot a half a block away. Mason had taken point on the other side of the abandoned ice cream shop, in someone's backyard.

Evie drove into the parking lot and got out of the car. She walked up to the Igloo Hut, and sat down cross-legged at the entrance of the drive-thru. She placed the gym bag and a can of gasoline onto the ground beside her.

"She's amazing," Mason breathed through Aiden's earbuds. Aiden kept his phone clipped to his jacket, his binoculars trained on Evie and his gun in his hand.

"Show me the passports," a man yelled out.

"He yelled from my side," Mason said. Aiden knew his lieutenant would run the asshole to ground, but there would probably be more than one.

"These might be your passports, they might not," she yelled out. She then proceeded to pour miniscule amounts of gas onto the gym bag, not enough to totally douse the contents, but enough for the bag to catch fire, it if were to be touched by flame.

"Stop that!" the voice yelled.

Mason went off at a run

She pulled a passport out of the bag and lifted it high above her. She then took a barbeque grill lighter and snapped it on, the flame burned bright in the late afternoon light. She set the flame against the passport and grinned as it burst into flames. She tossed it onto the ground.

She yelled out, "I'll burn them all if you don't show yourself and tell me where my sister and niece are."

"Step away from the passports."

Evie pulled out another passport and touched the flame to it.

A shot rang out, Evie ducked, but was she hit? Aiden was on the run towards her.

As Aiden crossed the street to get to her, he saw Evie get up and grab the gym bag. What the fuck? She started running to the back of the restaurant. That's when Aiden saw a man coming from behind the truck that Evie had driven. He veered towards him, and caught him in a flying tackle as he raised his gun.

"I yield," the man said immediately. Aiden straddled him, listening to the man with the English accent saying that he yielded. He hit him in the jaw. There was no way he was going to get out of this without a great deal of pain.

"I yield."

"I heard you," Aiden said through gritted teeth. He grabbed the man by the hair and knocked his head into the cement.

Out of the corner of his eye he saw the man fumbling with something in his left hand. It wasn't a gun, because that was now in Evie's hands as she held it trained on the asshole.

"I'll kill them right now. I'll blow them to bits."

Aiden stopped mid-thunk. He released the man's head. "What are you talking about?"

"I have the detonator. Give me the passports, or I'll press this button and blow them sky high."

Aiden looked at the tiny remote control in the man's hands. He was almost one hundred percent sure it wasn't an issue. Drake and Clint would have had enough time to rescue Trend and Bella, but he couldn't risk it. He got up off Khalid.

The man pushed himself off the cement and lunged for the bag that was hanging off Evie's shoulder. It fell to the ground, and newspaper began to fly out of the bag.

"No!" he screamed in anguish. "No! No! No!"

"All of our plans!" Aiden saw the man's thumb move to push the button, but before he could Aiden tried to stop him. He aimed for his head and squeezed the trigger, the man's head exploded. Evie followed him to the ground. Her finger's clawed at his hand.

"Aiden? Aiden? Did he press the button?"

* * *

It seemed like forever before she heard Drake's voice come over Aiden's phone.

"Baby Girl, they're fine. They're alive."

As she wiped away her tears of joy, she realized her fingers were covered in blood. Khalid's blood, maybe even blood from the man she'd killed at the cabin. She held up her hand to show Aiden. He pulled up the hem of his shirt and immediately started to wipe away the blood and tears from her face.

"I need to see them."

"We'll get you there," Mason assured her. Aiden helped to her feet. If it hadn't been for him, she wouldn't have made it the few yards to the truck.

"He's dead? He's really dead?"

"Yes," Aiden murmured into her hair.

"They're safe?"

"Yes, Bella and Trenda are safe."

Her brain kicked in. "Where's Zoe?"

"I don't know. We'll find out," Aiden assured her.

On the way to Trenda's house, Mason's phone rang, and Mason put it on speaker. It was Clint.

"Apparently, Bella answered Trenda's phone. She told Khalid they were at a motel and he was able to figure out where they were," Clint explained.

Evie rested her head against Aiden's shoulder and sighed. All of this because Bella had liked to play with her mother's phone.

"Mase, the mission went like clockwork. We were able to disarm the device, and get the C-4 out of the house."

"How are they?" Evie asked as she lifted her head.

Clint took a long moment before he answered. "I'm not going to lie. It's going to take a while for them to get over this. They need to see you, Evie. You'll be able to help them."

Aiden squeezed her hand.

As soon as they were at her sister's house, he had the truck door open for her, and she flew up the steps to be with her sister. He was at her side. She pushed at the screen door, and she heard Bella's frantic screams. What was going on?

"My hair. My hair. My hair."

She skidded to a halt to the scene in the kitchen, Aiden and Mason not far behind her. Drake was holding a struggling Bella. Trenda looked like she was in a trance. Evie saw that there was silver duct tape still hanging from the two kitchen chairs, and Clint was finishing the job of cutting Trenda's feet free. Bella had been taped to the chair with the booster seat, and it was clear that some of her hair had been cut away with the tape since the long locks were dangling from the chair.

"Evie!" Bella screeched. "My hair!" She almost twisted out of Drake's arms. Evie held out her hands and Drake transferred her.

"It's okay, Baby, you look beautiful."

"I want my hair back," she sobbed.

"You'll look beautiful like the Owies do," Evie's reassured her. Bella sniffed.

Drake cupped the back of the toddler's head. "It'll grow back," he crooned. It was the wrong thing to say, she started to sob again. As soon as she mentioned the 'Owies' Evie wanted to know where Zoe was. She looked frantically around the room and her eyes lit on Lydia.

"Where's Zoe?" Lydia came up to her with a concerned expression.

"I'm sorry, I should have said something immediately." Aiden, who had his arm around Evie, looked up at the same time she did. Drake took Bella. "It's okay, Baby Girl, it's good news," her brother said as he took Bella back.

"Zoe was with a guy named Clive. She got to the cabin when the ambulance arrived for Chloe. They're at the hospital with Maddie, right now."

"Chloe's in the hospital?" Trenda asked.

Evie looked over and saw Trenda was still sitting in the chair. Mason was crouching beside her, he had his arm around her, trying to help her to her feet. Trenda stumbled upwards. "Take it slow," he murmured.

"We have to get to the hospital," Evie looked up to Aiden.

"Yes, we do," he said as he glanced down at her, and then over to Trenda and Bella.

"My hair," Bella whimpered one last time.

Evie looked at Trenda and saw that she still wasn't in any shape to cope with her daughter, so she held out her arms for Drake to give her the little girl.

"I want my hair, Auntie Evie." She looked up at her with tears in her eyes.

"Do you know what I want?" Evie asked.

"No," Bella said, her lip trembling.

"I want you to smile. How about we both go get haircuts tomorrow, and we'll look like the Owies."

Bella fingered Evie's long hair. "We'll be pretty?"

"You'll be the most gorgeous women imaginable," Aiden promised.

Epilogue

Aiden watched Evie hang up her phone, and then trace the face of it with her fingers. She did this every time she was done with her nightly calls to Tennessee. He wondered if the other women did something similar. It had been three weeks since that harrowing afternoon. She still wasn't remembering things the way everybody else did, and he was determined to put a stop to it tonight.

He slid open the door to the deck, and sat down behind her on the oversized deck chair. She leaned back against him, her short hair skimming her jaw.

"I thought you were going to be late," she murmured.

"I had a vision of you out here alone, at dusk, and decided to come home sooner." He brushed a kiss against her temple. "How are the girls?" He flicked his fingers toward the phone.

"Maddie and Zoe are fine. Chloe's lying to me and saying she's fine, but Zoe's ratting her out. Maddie and Zoe are going to double team her and get her into counselling."

That was a new and welcome piece of information. "And Trenda?"

"Bella's night terrors are getting worse. She's taken her to a child psychologist, but nothing has helped."

"Is Trenda talking to Bella about how she feels?"

Evie twisted around in the chair so she could look at Aiden. Even in the dim light he could see the anguish in her face. "Trenda's blocked most of it. When I ask her about that day, she can't seem to recollect it. She says it's like a bad dream. She uses words like hazy and blurry. Sometimes, I think we Avery girls bury stuff we can't handle."

Aiden snorted. But it wasn't funny. "She's got to get that shit sorted out for Bella's sake."

"She knows that. She's talking about seeing a hypnotherapist if necessary. She'd give up her life for Bella."

He kissed the top of Evie's head. "I know that, Kitten."

He took a deep breath and blew it out.

"What?"

"You don't talk about that day either."

Evie went stiff in his arms. "Sure, I do. I fell apart. I screamed, and cried, and threw up. I was a fucking mess."

"You killed a man."

"It was a lucky swing." She tried to get off the chair.

"According to Lydia, that guy would have ended up killing her if it hadn't been for you."

"Yeah, yeah. She's said that before. That's bullshit." Evie wiggled more. She was damn near struggling to get out of Aiden's arms, but he wouldn't let her go.

"Here are the facts, Evie. Are you ready to listen?"

"Because of me one sister got beaten, and my other sister and niece almost got blown up. I know the facts." She wrenched out of his arms and scrambled off the chair and lunged into the house. He followed her.

"You can't help what some madman did."

Evie was at the refrigerator pulling out a beer. "I'm going to have one. Maybe two or six. Better get one now before they're all gone," she said bitterly. She took a long swig.

"Listen to me," Aiden begged.

"No! Why do you keep harping on this?"

"You just said that the Avery girls bury things, didn't you? You said that Maddie and Zoe are going to drag Chloe to counselling. You killed a man that day. Do you think you don't have any psychological scars? Evie, I love you to death, but you're seriously fucked in the head about this."

"Nice, Aiden. Real nice." She slammed down the beer bottle.

"For three weeks, I've tried nice. I thought I would try 'Avery Speak.'

"So hit me. Give it to me straight, Doc. After all, you're a medic."

"Sit down on the couch."

"No. I'll stand for this." He squeezed the bridge of his nose. She was such a stubborn wench.

"Did the guy you kill almost have his gun out of the shoulder holster? Just answer yes or no."

"Lydia would have-"

"Yes or no."

"Yes. But Lydia would have shot him in time."

"She says she wouldn't have, are you calling her a liar?" He pinned her gaze. She glanced down at the floor.

"No, she's not a liar."

"Okay, you saved her life. That's point one."

Evie glared at him.

"Whose idea was it to have Maddie go to the back of the house and distract them so you two could kill those fuckers?"

"Lydia would have come up with it."

"Just answer the Goddamn question."

"Mine."

"That's point two."

"I didn't get it done in time, Chloe was still beaten."

"Is she dead?" Aiden asked relentlessly.

Evie finally shook her head 'no.'

"That's point three. And then there's the point I really want to make. The point that abso-fucking-lutely amazes me."

Evie looked up at him with a dazed expression.

"Somehow, when you get a call from a man who tortured you, a man who has your sister and her baby, you have the balls and intelligence to lie and negotiate with him, even when he drops you to your knees. I loved you before that, but after that, I worshiped you."

Aiden watched as tears dripped down her face.

"I could have gotten them killed," she stuttered. "I was bluffing. I didn't know what I was doing."

"Nobody could have done better than you did."

"I threw up."

"Most men would have shit their pants. But not my Avery girl. She got the job done."

Evie stood in the kitchen, shudders coursing through her body.

"Did you hear me this time? Did it get through that head of yours that you're a fucking hero?"

"I'm not."

Aiden pulled out his Navy SEAL Trident pin and pulled her close. He pinned it on her collar. "Yes. Yes, you are a hero."

She collapsed in his arms.

* * *

Evie wasn't even sure how she ended up in their bedroom, or how much time had passed, all she knew is that she was surrounded by a man who represented safety, security, home.

"Aiden."

"What, Eva?

"Just Aiden. I whisper your name sometimes. It makes me happy."

In the moonlight, his lips found hers. Whisper soft.

"I can't take your pin."

"You're a hero, aren't you?"

She smiled. A real smile, from the heart. He saw it. She got another kiss.

She'd be putting his pin back on his uniform in the morning, but his gesture? She'd never forget the moment when he pinned that on her collar. Her eyes had finally opened.

"I love you, Aiden. Every day, every night, you give me something new to hold onto."

His arm curled behind her back and pulled her high so that she was looking directly into the dark blue depths of his eyes.

"Make no mistake, Eva, I am never letting you go. So, you go right on ahead and hold on tight. This is a ride that is going to last to the end of this life and beyond."

She hooked her arms around his neck and took a deep breath. The scent of her man. Aiden. Safety. Love.

Evie trailed kisses up his jaw and then their lips met.

It was an explosion of want and need.

Tongues tangling, she arched into his hold, and gloried in the feel of his big hand cupping her breast, his thumb caressing her nipple through her blouse.

"More," she panted as she fumbled for the buttons of her top.

"Be still." He pushed her down on the bed and took long minutes uncovering her flesh to his heated gaze.

"Hurry," she begged as she clawed at the collar of his shirt. Finally he relented and stood up beside the bed. The best part of the night started as he stripped.

"You're gorgeous, you know that don't you?" Even in the dim light she could see him flush. He opened the nightstand, his hand hesitating.

"What?" she asked.

"Eventually, I want six daughters. No son, just six daughters who look like you."

Evie gut clenched. "I want boys and I want them blond. But we need to practice."

He knelt on the bed and whispered in her ear. "We have time, first I want a few years with just us."

"A year," she negotiated.

He slid between her legs and she sighed with pleasure. She bent her knees and caught him closer, their hands clutching at one another as he thrust and she arched. He kissed her throat and she scraped her nails up his spine, he plunged deep and she moaned her pleasure.

"Please, just a little more," she begged.

He lifted his head and laughed. One last push and she careened off into space. She heard him shout her name and she sighed, contented, then fell into a blissful sleep.

* * *

"Aiden Carlos, she's precious. I'm happy now."

Aiden woke with a start. He looked down at Evie, she was sound asleep. He listened to her even breathing. This time he recognized the woman's voice. It was his mother's.

He looked out the window and saw the vast expanse of sky. "I love you, Mom." He whispered. Then he quietly got out of bed and went to his office. He had a phone call to make.

"Did you get it done?" Drake asked.

Aiden had snuck out of their bedroom after Evie fell asleep to call her brother.

"Yes. I think it finally worked. I think she finally gets that she was incredible that day."

"Thank fuck. Good job, man."

"That's not the reason I'm calling, though."

"What then?" Drake asked.

"I want your permission to marry Evie."

There was a long pause. Aiden didn't take it personally, he knew this was gravely important.

"Be good to her, Aiden. She deserves the sun and the moon."

"I know. I'm going to do my best to give them to her."

The End

BIOGRAPHY

Caitlyn O'Leary is an avid reader, and considers herself a fan first and an author second. She reads a wide variety of genres, but finds herself going back to happily-ever-afters. Getting a chance to write, after years in corporate America, is a dream come true. She hopes her stories provide the kind of entertainment and escape she has found from some of her favorite authors.

Keep up with Caitlyn O'Leary:

Facebook: http://tinyurl.com/nuhvey2
Twitter: http://twitter.com/CaitlynOLearyNA
Pinterest: http://tinyurl.com/q36uohc
Goodreads: http://tinyurl.com/nqy66h7
Website: http://www.caitlynoleary.com
Email: caitlyn@caitlynoleary.com
Newsletter: http://bit.ly/1WIhRup
Instagram: http://bit.ly/29WaNIh

BOOKS BY CAITLYN O'LEARY

The Found Series

Revealed, Book One
Forsaken, Book Two
Healed, Book Three
Beloved, Book Four (Coming Soon)

Midnight Delta Series

Midnight Delta Box Set Volume One (Books 1-5)
Her Vigilant SEAL, Book One
Her Loyal SEAL, Book Two
Her Adoring SEAL, Book Three
SEALed with a Kiss, A Midnight Delta Novella, Book Four
Her Daring SEAL, Book Five
Her Fierce SEAL, Book Six
Protecting Hope, Book Seven
(Seal of Protection & Midnight Delta Crossover Novel
Susan Stoker KindleWorld)
A SEAL's Vigilant Heart, Book Eight
Her Dominant SEAL, Book Nine
Her Relentless SEAL, Book Ten

Shadow Alliance

Declan, Book One
Cooper's Promise, Book Two
(Omega Team and Shadow Alliance Crossover Novel
Desiree Holt KindleWorld)

Fate Harbor Series Published by Siren/Bookstrand

Trusting Chance, Book One
Protecting Olivia, Book Two
Claiming Kara, Book Three
Isabella's Submission, Book Four
Cherishing Brianna, Book Five

Printed in Great Britain
by Amazon